Ode to Rebellion

A. M. Harris

Credits
Cover Artist: Designs by Ms G
Editor: Sherry Derr-Wille

Dedication

For my 7th-grade reading teacher: You may be the dream crusher, but you didn't crush my dreams. Thank you for the homework.

Prologue

The explosions ring in my ears as they light up the Council Dwellings. In brief flashes of red glow I see the building, standing regally and impenetrable to all whom tried to pierce its walls. That was until tonight when we began the siege on the pearly gates that held the beating hearts of Ode's Council. For the first time in the history of Ode, the Council Dwellings will fall.

Its tall gleaming pillars, cascading staircase, cavernous domes and unprotected ornate doors will no longer be under the control of the elite Council. They will belong to the common Oderian, paid for in full with blood. In another flash of light, I see the staircase, littered with the broken bodies of those who have been slain. The blood runs like a raging river from the top of the staircase, staining the once crisp white stairs with a violet hue. My eyes follow the bloody river down to the bottom of the staircase where my breath gets caught in my throat.

There, at the bottom of the staircase, surrounded by an ocean of blood, stands the gallows; the ropes swinging ominously in the breeze. The wood creaks with every gust, mimicking the soft pleas for help from its victims. After noticing the freshly tied rope, I feel my neck tighten and my lungs gasp for the air they most desperately need. I can almost feel the coarse rope pulling tighter and tighter until...Pop. The victim's neck snaps if they were lucky, those who weren't, were strangled to death.

My mother had been one of those souls stolen by the dreaded noose. She was taken away from me when I was young. The memories are like a blur in my head. All I remember are pieces, fragments of joyous memories, her features, her gentle touch, and an Earthly lullaby coaxing me to sleep. These are all I have left of my mother before the Council arrested her. Before they hanged her for a crime she didn't commit.

I was once told about the drastic change when humans arrived here, three hundred sixty moons ago. However, it was far before my time. I do know something like this has never happened before on Ode. We are peaceful and cooperative people, a government takeover, followed by a mass rebellion, then genocide. This is unheard of for us. Many blame the influence of humans because of their violent past, but I have never met a cruel human, my mother was human. She could never hurt anyone. With the blame stuck on humans and their children, many wish for them to leave. They cannot return to Earth. Although Earth still exists, it is uninhabitable by life. Nova has pointed it out for me in our sky many times.

The aching in my hearts grows ever stronger. It doesn't go away now. It stays with me, following me like my shadow. I'm unable to run from it, and unable to hide from it. It's impossible to get even a brief moment of relief.

Now I know what Nova felt like, dragging me into his world. A world full of blood, pain, and death. A world where there is no happiness, just the shadows you can't run from. He was scared. He knew something like this would happen. He knew at some point I would have to face his world without him by my side.

I step away from the Commanders and look down as I blink back tears. I study my shaking blue hands. I sit down and lay back on the ground. My silver eyes take in the site above me, so many stars, so many beautiful stars. They look like the ones Nova showed me a few moons ago.

Nova would never have wanted this to happen. He would never have wanted me to put myself in danger, at least without him there to help me...to protect me.

I glance around me at the other Oderians, their light blue skin glows intensely as they prepare themselves for what may very well be their last day. A few humans stand alongside them in the dark, about to fight a battle, millions of miles from their planet of origin, in a place unfamiliar to them.

This place doesn't seem familiar to me anymore. These are not the same people I knew when I was young. It was so different before all this started. My days were all the same and I would wish for an adventure to break the painstaking repetitiveness of my life. Now, I wish this nightmare would end. There has been enough adventure, action, death, pain, and worry in the past few moons to last me a lifetime.

Sadly, I could never be lucky enough for something like that to happen. There will be plenty more death and pain in my future, it's impossible to avoid.

Shaking my head as I stand, I glance up at the Council Dwellings. I hate them. I hate this government. I hate them for putting me into this position, for taking my family, for taking Nova's family, but I hate them most of all for taking Nova from me. He was all I had left in this strange new world. He was my one friend. He was my lifeline and shock of reality.

This is the first time I've left the base since Nova's disappearance. He said it was one of the few places where we could be safe from the Council. He was wrong at times, but for the most part we were safe there while he taught me. Giving me every chance at life he possibly could, he is the reason why I'm still living and breathing now. From the day all of this began, to when he was taken, he did everything to keep me safe, no matter if he put himself in danger in the process. He was there from day one.

I smile to myself as I remember that typical day.

Chapter One

Ara

My regeneration tube vibrates softly telling me it's time to get up and get the day moving.

I groan as I wobbly stand, maybe going for a run with Nova yesterday wasn't such a good idea. My legs ache so intensely I sit right back down again. I shake them out, trying to get the pain to ease.

I glance around my room as I do this. Constellations decorate the walls and ceiling. For some reason ever since Nova started teaching me about them, I've been obsessed with stars and the way people like to make pictures out of them. I remember the time Nova told me how the constellations received their names. He said thousands of years ago there was a group of people who lived on Earth, they were called the Greeks. They believed there were gods who controlled what happened in the world around them, they also believed there were demigods, children of the gods and mortals. Many constellations were named after the gods, demigods and the monsters they battled in the myths. My favorites are Hercules and Pegasus, even though they are very faint in our sky.

I look over at another wall and see my staff hanging in its case. Every Oderian is given one when they are born, whether they ever use it is up to them. I've never used mine because I have never been presented with the chance to do so, and I hope I never will. The red glass globe shimmers in the light. I could stare at it for hours, the swirls and color patterns never seeming to end.

Suddenly there is a knock at the door of my room, startling me from my thoughts.

"Come in." I sigh as I stretch my stiff and sore body.

The person outside the door clicks the button and the door slides open with a quiet whoosh. I glance up and see Nova grinning at me. I give him a cheesy grin right back.

"Did you get up a few moments ago?" he asks as he strolls into the room. Nova leans against the side of my regeneration tube as I try to stand up again.

"I'm trying to. It's not so easy when your entire body feels like it's on fire," I groan as my spine crackles.

Nova nods. "Get ready quickly 'cause we're going for another run today."

"Do we have to?" I whine.

He laughs and replies, "Yes, you have too. If not then we will go on two tomorrow." For a moment he traces the constellations on my walls, "They never get old do they?"

I shake my head, "No, they never do and they never will. They are constantly changing after all."

"They are," he nods. "I'll let you get ready for our run now so you will quit purposely stalling."

I pout. "How did you figure it out?"

"It's not very difficult." He leaves the room so I can change, but I know he is standing right outside the door.

"I don't know how long I'm going to be able to run today. I'm still really sore from yesterday," I say as I slip off my plain white regeneration clothes and put on my Tan Dew, the traditional clothing for Oderians. I should be getting new colors soon, every moon we get a new Tan Dew in a different color which represents our age. I lace up what many humans call a corset, however here on Ode they provide protection for our hearts.

"Eventually you'll get used to it and you won't get sore anymore," Nova explains as I push the button on the door and it slides open. "Besides if you miss today then you will be behind and it will take you longer to adjust to the running and the exercise."

I glance around and see him leaning against the wall, right next to the door. "Fine, I guess I have to."

"Are you ready?" he asks as he stands up straight and follows me down the hall. I glance back at him, for some reason his cloak always seems to billow out behind him as he walks, making him seem so regal and important.

"I am but first I want to get something to eat." After searching around for something, I come up empty handed.

"Looking for this?"

I whip around and see Nova holding up a small package, a nutrition bar made especially for Oderians. I eat one every day and he knows that. Nova enjoys messing with me. It has become a tradition of his to do odd things whenever possible.

"Hey," I exclaim as I snatch the bar from Nova and walk out of the house.

As I chew, Nova comes up behind me and asks, "How are you coping? It's been several moons since the Council imprisoned your father."

"I'm okay, I guess. I've been finding ways to distract myself. I get upset if I dwell on it for too long," I answer in between bites.

Nova shrugs his shoulders, "Understandable. Have you heard anything else about what happened?"

"They won't tell me anything. It's so confusing. One moment, my father is the most loved and reasonable member of the Council, the next moment the entire planet hates him for something he probably didn't do," I shake my head as I respond. "Plus, ever since the whole thing happened, it's like no one wants to even be associated with me. I'll walk up to the Council dwellings and the whole way there, no one will even look at me. Not to mention how being a hybrid makes everything even more difficult."

Nova sighs, "It's all probably the Council, I bet they cooked up some crazy rumor about you so no one would want to be around you."

I laugh a little and reply, "I wouldn't be surprised. They are always cooking something up." I finish my food and turn back to Nova. "Thus, the reason why I am always alone. Hey, did you hear about the murder of those two hybrids by a group of Constables?"

Nova pales slightly. "I did."

"I can understand why you are scared, Nova." I sigh as I see his expression.

"Y-you can?" he stutters, surprised.

"Yes, however, I am not scared because I have you with me. I am a hybrid, I am proud and I have a very close friend who will keep me safe from any monstrous Constables," I answer, smiling brightly at him.

"Yes, I wouldn't let any of them hurt you," Nova nods, suddenly at ease again. I wonder what that was about.

"Are we going to go for a run or not?" I ask.

He grins, acting completely different than he had been a few moments ago, "Try to keep up." He takes off and I go after him, laughing as I run.

I squint as I glance up at the lilac colored sky. The seven suns seem to be brighter than ever today. Usually, they are much dimmer and we have to rely more on our glow to see anything, even then our sightline is limited. Sightline is nothing for me though. I have to rely on other Oderians' glows because I can't glow. No hybrid can as far as I know. However, there have been stories about how some hybrids started glowing during an extreme situation. It makes life harder for hybrids as if we didn't already have a hard-enough time.

The thumping of my boots comes to a stop as I stand still and stare at the sky.

"Are you alright Ara?" Nova asks as he doubles back to see what I am doing.

"I'm looking at the sky," I answer.

"It's not nearly as interesting during the day as it is at night when all the stars have come out." Nova stares up at the sky with me for a moment.

For some reason, I feel like something is off, like how my mother told me about the calm before the storm. How the feeling in your bones told you the storm was coming but outside everything was still, there was no wind, the sun shone, everything was serene. Then a few hours later the wind would be coming in gusts and the rain was pounding on everything.

"You are alright, correct?" Nova asks his question again.

I shake my head, clearing my thoughts, "I'm fine."

"Okay," Nova says suspiciously, "Are you sure?

"Yes, I'm sure. Now let's go." I take off running again. The thumping of my boots in time with the thumps of my hearts is loud in my ears.

I run until my lungs burn for air and my legs feel like liquid. I drop to the ground, lying on my back as my chest heaves sucking in and pushing out air at a rapid pace.

"Good job, Ara." Nova stops beside me, not even short of breath. He stares down at me trying to keep from laughing at my exhausted state.

"Easy...for you...to say," I gasp, still trying to catch my breath. "Literally, because you...can talk..." I heave, "I...can't."

He laughs as he reaches out a hand to help me up. I gladly take it and he pulls me to my feet. I glance up at his face. He's quite a bit taller than me and he has built up a decent amount of muscle.

"You did excellent, though," he says as I take off my cloak and brush the dirt off of it. At the moment my Tan Dew has a blue color scheme. My shirt and pants are a slightly lighter blue than the cloak. He helps me brush off more of the dust so we can head back a little quicker.

I shrug, finally starting to catch my breath. "I guess these runs are really hard on the lungs."

"Your lungs will get stronger the more you run, the same goes for your legs," Nova answers as I pull the cloak back around my neck. He helps me refasten it around my shoulders.

"Sometimes I wonder why you put up with me Nova," I sigh as we start walking back to where I live.

"If I didn't then who would?" He laughs as I roll my eyes. Leave it to Nova to try and make it a joke. "No, but really I put up with you because you are willing to put up with me. It's a mutual put up with each other kind of relationship," he says as his grin fades into a small smile. "Why would it matter? What is going on with you today? You seem..." he pauses, "Off."

"I feel like something is off. Me, the rest of the world, I

don't know but it's strange. You know how sometimes you feel like something really bad is going to happen. You don't know what, so you sit wondering what it is and how bad it's going to be." I scuff my feet as I talk, sending a small cloud of dirt into the air. I cough slightly on it, quickly regretting kicking the ground.

Nova nods, not fazed by the cloud of dirt. "I get that feeling a lot. I don't mean to scare you, but usually that feeling is right."

~ * ~

Nova and I lie on the roof of my home and stare up at the stars above us. He points to random constellations, quizzing me on them.

"That one?"

"Camelopardalis," I answer.

"And that one?" he points to another.

"Vela," I say quickly.

"How about that one?" he asks.

"Lyra." I sigh.

"You are getting much better," he nods, turning from the sky to look at me. His smile seems to brighten his glow.

"Who taught you all the human's constellations?" I ask as I turn from the stars to look at him. His smile quickly falls at my question and he reverts his eyes back up to the stars.

"I learned about them a long time ago from a friend of mine. He had a human sickness which was incurable, even by us. He passed away many moons ago," Nova mumbles.

"Oh," I say. "I'm sorry I asked."

"No, it's all right." Nova shakes his head. "So, in his memory, I learned everything I could about the stars. I even learned where most of the constellations originated back on Earth."

"It makes me wonder why Ode had no interest in stars. There is so much more out there, we know now because the humans have come here," I whisper.

"I know. It makes me wonder what other amazing things we could find if we explored a little like they did."

Nova agrees, he turns to look at me once more.

"Can you imagine leaving your home planet forever, though? They will never see the places they grew up ever again," I ask him, turning to lie on my side to face him.

"I couldn't, even though there are places here I never want to see again. There are far too many of those, but still, I don't think I could ever pack up and leave Ode. It's my home whether I like it or not." Nova looks back to the stars.

I stare at him for a moment, his glow giving me a warm comfort in the cool dark night. I still have the feeling deep down something big is about to happen. I wish the feeling would go away. I don't look forward to whatever it is because it's not going to be good.

Maybe my subconscious is trying to tell me I forgot something I will need later. I don't know.

Chapter Two

Ara

"Hey, Nova where are you?" I ask as I walk through the learning center. Nova and I often meet here. Many come to the free classes taught by Oderian elders. Oderians love to learn, most of us strive for enlightenment.

I walk into the room Nova and I usually meet in as I ponder this. I find the room pitch black and Nova lying on the floor staring at the ceiling.

"What are you doing?" I ask.

"Come and lay down." He pats the floor next to him.

I lie down on the floor next to him and hear a click. Suddenly, the ceiling lights up. I see stars and constellations. I also see how Nova is wearing new colors. His shirt is white and his pants and cloak are black. His new cuirass shines in the dim light. It matches his cloak in the rich black.

"How many moons did you turn?" I ask him.

"Two hundred and forty moons today," he answers still looking at the stars.

"Your new cuirass is amazing," I murmur.

He nods and grins, "It's strong too. My old one was getting weak. They decided my hearts were in danger, so they gave me a new one. Go ahead, hit it."

I quickly take him up on his offer. I slam my fist into the new cuirass, yelp in pain, then pull away nursing my hand.

"Didn't feel a thing," he says, nodding in amusement.

"You didn't, but I did," I squeak, as I try and shake the pain away.

Nova turns back to the projection of stars, pointing to one. "That one is Ode, and that one," he points to another star far from Ode. "That one is Earth."

I nod slowly. "Earth is so far away," I sigh.

"Yep," he agrees.

We both jump when the projection screen suddenly turns itself on and the room lights up. I cringe and squint at the screen as my eyes try to adjust to the sudden flood of bright lights.

"All Oderians need to report to The Council Dwellings. This is mandatory. I repeat all Oderians need to report to the Council Dwellings. This is mandatory," says a man with a deep voice. Nova suddenly jumps to his feet, pulling me up with him.

I look up at Nova, confused. "I didn't know there was a meeting today."

He looks down at me, his expression full of concern. "I want you to run, now. Grab anything important to you and meet me down the street," he says, as he starts looking around the room, gathering up his things.

"Why?" I ask, still very confused.

"Go and hurry," he exclaims, grabbing me by the shoulders, spinning me around and pushing me out the door.

"I-Okay." I give up trying to ask any questions. I'm obviously not going to get an answer right now.

I race out of the learning center, running to my house. I grab a bag, stuffing things in it. I stuff a couple changes of clothes, a few cloaks, and a regeneration kit in case someone gets hurt. I pause, thinking for a second, I don't know how long we will be gone. I race down the stairs and grab several nutrition bars and put them in the bag.

What is going on? I ask myself. *Is this why I had the weird feeling that something bad was going to happen? Is this the bad situation?*

I grab a few other items I deem important, but then I stop. *What about my father?* I ask myself. *If this is as dire a situation as Nova makes out, what will he do? He is stuck in the hands of the Council. He can't escape even if his life depends on it. Maybe he could find a way. He would probably be worried about me...No, he knows I would be with Nova. Nova would never leave my side.*

I shake my head clear of these thoughts and race out of the house. I meet Nova down the street.

"Did you get everything you needed?" he asks.

I glance down at my bag, "I believe so."

"Then come on," he starts walking.

"Nova?" I ask.

"Yes?"

"Is this a life or death situation?" I inquire.

"It may be," he answers.

"Then where is your family?" I stop walking as I ask him.

He pauses his stride for a moment. "No longer here," he responds with hurt in his eyes. "Let's go." Suddenly, he starts heading down the street again.

I quickly chase after him.

"Nova, are you alright?" I ask him after I catch up. I set my hand on his shoulder. He shrugs me off and keeps walking.

I catch up to him again grabbing him by the shoulders, turning him towards me. "Are you alright, Nova?" I ask him again. "I know how you get when you are upset about something. You are either really quiet like you are now, or you're yelling at something. Now, talk to me because I would prefer you yelling to you being completely silent. You have been entirely too silent and that scares me."

He glares down at me, his face set in a deep frown. "I'm fine Ara. Let's get going." Brushing my question off, he takes my hand and continues walking.

I sigh, giving up once again on trying to get any information out of him, "Where are we going anyway?"

"You'll find out when we get there," he replies, not even looking back at me.

Chapter Three

Ara

Nova leads me to a small building in a secluded area, one of the few areas I know of where plants can actually grow. Most of Ode is flat and there is little vegetation, but the planet makes up for the small amount of vegetation with large pockets of oxygen. The oxygen gets released into the air with loud explosions.

I follow him into the building, and I find the building filled with humans, Oderians, and hybrids. Everyone is crowded together, and the room is several degrees warmer than outside because of all the bodies.

I look around as Nova pulls me to the front of the small room. He weaves through the crowd. Some people part almost immediately, recognition on their faces as he walks by.

"Why are we here?" I ask Nova, trying once again to get some kind of information out of him.

"You will find out here in a moment," he answers as we get to the front of the room.

Nova glances around as if looking for someone. I look around also, trying once more to figure out what is going on. "There," he sighs, then starts toward a human standing in the corner of the room, looking around nervously. The man is short and stocky. He wouldn't stand out in a crowd. His hair looks unkempt and thinning, scruff grows on his chin. His Tan Dew is ragged and dirty, his cuirass scratched and worn. Something terrible must have happened to him. Nova leads me up to him.

"You made it," the man exclaims joyously as he claps Nova on the shoulder.

"Of course," Nova responds, nodding toward the man in acknowledgment. "With so much at stake, I would never miss this. I assume you haven't started the fun yet?"

The man glances away and frowns. "I'll start all that here in a minute. I truly don't look forward to it. I'm about to destroy quite a few people's lives. Many of them won't even survive through this moon, let alone through the war which is about to happen."

I turn away from Nova and the man; glancing around the room I see people hugging each other, while others seem panicked. *What is going on? Why are people freaking out? What are Nova and the strange man talking about?*

They shake hands, "Once again, thank you for coming. You will be very important in these upcoming moons." The man suddenly steps away from Nova and me. He glances down at his cuirass and straightens it slightly, before reaching up and combing through his hair with his fingers. He gets up in front of everyone, motioning for the crowd to sit down in the dirt.

Everyone sits as the roar of the crowd dies down to a soft lull of whispers and nervous glances.

The man looks around, a grim expression set on his face. "My good friends..." he starts and the crowd goes quiet. "As you know The Council is having everyone meet in the dwellings."

People nod, motioning for him to go on, some anxious to find out what is happening.

"We are not there for a reason. I called you here to tell you, the Council is turning on us," the man states.

The crowd suddenly starts murmuring to each other, conversing and trying to figure out what the man means by this statement. He twiddles his thumbs nervously, glancing around at the reactions of the crowd.

My own reaction surprises me. The beating of my hearts suddenly speeds up, my eyes widen and I look to Nova. How could The Council turn on us? Why would they ever turn on their own people?

My mind whirls at the endless possibilities until it suddenly stops. My father.

Whatever this is, he would have opposed it. He would never turn on the people who love and adore him. This must be the reason why they made up something to get rid of him. They had plotted the whole thing out. Their entire plan was to dispose of him so they could go through with their own agenda. Why didn't I see it before? It should have been obvious. My poor father probably knew he would be imprisoned. He knew this was going to happen. He didn't even bother to warn me. He let it happen, let me watch as my father, the last of my family, was taken from me. How could he have put me through this? I thought he was a good man.

I get pulled back into reality as the man starts to speak again, "Do not let this disaster steal your hope. There is a group of rebels who live in the mountains not far off, their base is safe and if you agree to their terms and help with the rebellion then you will be allowed to stay there. At the base, you will be protected, given lodging and food." He pauses looking around the room. "There is a caveat, however. They will make most of the able-bodied men and women fight. Unfortunately, my good friends, this may be the beginning of a very bloody war," he exclaims.

Chapter Four

Ara

I never, ever thought the council would turn on us. Questions continue to fly through my head. *Why does the Council want this? What is their ultimate plan?*

Suddenly, the feeling I had yesterday returns, the feeling that something really bad is about to happen and there is no way I could ever stop it.

Nova glances over at me seeing my confusion. "They are persecuting hybrids and those who support them."

I whip my head toward Nova and ask without even thinking first, "That's why your parents aren't here, right?" I immediately regret asking him right after I say it. It's really none of my business.

He nods his head solemnly, "They supported human, hybrid and Oderian interactions."

I frown as I wrap my arms around him, hugging him tightly, "I'm so sorry. I shouldn't have asked. So much is happening right now, I can barely think."

"It's alright Ara. I'll be fine." Nova replies flatly, pulling away from me.

He has never been much of a physical affection kind of person. He glances down to his hands for a moment. I know he won't be alright for quite a long while, and he won't ever forgive himself for leaving them alone.

"I need to explain something to you, Ara," Nova says, looking back up at me.

"Go ahead." I motion for him to go on and speak.

"I talked to your father before the Council imprisoned him," he sighs, slightly apprehensive.

"Okay..." I trail off, confused.

"He knew this was coming, he told me to keep you safe," Nova states.

"He knew this was coming? Why didn't he tell me?" I ask. More of the questions from a few moments ago return, and even more begin to form, but still, none of them get answered.

My father knew about this? He knew this was going to happen?

"He didn't tell you because he was afraid it would scare you. He thought he could stop the Council before they went through with it. Obviously, he failed. The Council figured out what he was up to and decided they needed to shut him up before he ruined their plans," Nova explains.

"That's why they sent him to prison," I nod, my hearts sinking in my chest.

"Yes, he gave me specific instructions. Should he fail, and should the Council go through with their plan, I need to take you somewhere safe," he continues.

"What about him? What will the Council do to him? What have they already done to him..." I trail off, getting distracted again.

"Ara, we need to leave so I can get you somewhere safe. The Council knows we are here and they are on the way right now. This is what your father wanted," Nova says.

I stare at him and reply, "How can we leave? The Council has my father. How can I leave him to go somewhere safe while he is still in danger? Besides, where would we go? How do we know which places are safe and which are not?"

"Ara, he wants you to leave so you are safe. Don't worry about him, your father is strong and will be able to take care of himself. I will be with you, so wherever we go will be safe," Nova sighs, getting frustrated.

"How do you know for sure? How are you supposed to fight the Constables who will inevitably come after us, because I am a hybrid," I exclaim.

"I will, it doesn't matter how," he replies.

"This is my life we are talking about. Hell, this is even your life we are talking about. I have seen the way those stupid Constables fight. Only other Constables even stand a chance. They have already killed hundreds of hybrids. It doesn't matter how old they are, who their parents are, or what part of Ode they are from! They will hunt us down and kill us both." My voice gets softer as I speak.

"Trust me Ara. There was a reason your father asked me to take care of you if this happened. I am doing what he wants. He knew what he was up against. He made sure he planned for the worst. This is the worst. Trust me, he plotted everything out," Nova explains. "Ultimately, it's up to you to decide what you want. This is what your father wanted though. I would advise you to make your decision quickly. We don't have much time before Constables show up here."

I sit and think for a second. "Fine, I will go with you if you help me find a way to stop the Council and rescue my father. I am not going to sit here and do nothing while the Council murders my father and all of the hybrids on Ode."

He frowns at me. "Alright," he huffs. "Now, let's get going before some…" He stops when there is a sudden loud banging on the door of the small building. He jumps to his feet, pulling me up with him. "Now we are really going to have to hurry. You should have made your decision faster."

Nova pushes me behind him, putting himself between me and the door. I can feel my stomach drop as I stare over his shoulder, wide-eyed, with fear coursing through my body. Nova doesn't take his eyes off the door as it rattles violently.

"Open up. By order of the Council, you must open this door or face the Council's wrath," a deep voice calls as the banging continues.

"Come on Ara, we have to go," Nova exclaims as he turns and starts trying to shove his way through the crowd. I am frozen with fear as Nova finally gets moving.

The banging on the door continues. Suddenly, the door flies open. There stands the Council Constables in dark blue uniforms with matching cuirasses.

"You have undermined the Council. Therefore, you must come with us to face your judgment for treason," a Constable at the front of the group says fiercely. The Constables take several steps forward into the room.

"The Council is willing to offer a reward for all hybrids. They must be turned over to the Council now," the Constable states.

Nova glances back and finds I hadn't moved. He quickly comes back, taking my hand tightly, but my feet are planted to the ground. I am too scared to move. I stare at the large staves the Constables carry, knowing they can easily kill someone with them.

"Come on Ara we need to leave, now," Nova exclaims in a whisper, tugging on my hand.

He pulls me to the ground and I turn to him, very confused, "How are we going to escape?"

"Follow me," he whispers. "Stay down. If they see you, they will try to take you with everyone else."

The crowd is constantly moving as people panic and try to escape the Constables. Mothers hold their children close, and husbands place themselves between the Constables and their families. We weave our way through the crowd of people, staying as close to the ground as possible.

"Almost there," Nova whispers back to me.

We pass by the man who spoke to Nova when we first arrived here. He nods to Nova, then gives me an encouraging smile. "Good luck," he whispers.

I can't believe this is happening. I am a wanted fugitive on the run from the Council. Was this really part of my father's plan to keep me safe?

Nova stops and starts brushing the dirt off of a square area.

"Is now really the time to be cleaning?" I ask. "We are trying to escape from some Constables, you know."

"I have to do this," Nova rolls his eyes

"What's down there then?" I ask quietly as I watch. I glance around at the panicking crowd.

"Our escape route," he answers, not even looking up at me.

I look around once again waiting for Nova to finish clearing the area. I notice how there aren't nearly as many people in here as there were earlier.

Then it hits me. The Constables must be pulling people out, looking for all the hybrids. We really need to hurry.

"I'm almost done," Nova says, noticing my worry.

Suddenly, someone yanks me to my feet and turns me around. I find myself face to face with a Constable. I stare at him, shaking with fear.

He grins horribly, "Look what I found. A hybrid."

I have heard horrible stories about the Constables, how they are very violent and can be angered very quickly. I've heard how they have killed innocent people. There have been stories about how hybrids have been found brutally murdered by Constables. I don't understand how someone could kill in cold blood like that. I believe they are unfeeling, cruel monsters. The one that's holding me though is definitely the worst. I bet his personality is about as ugly as his face is. It is littered with scars, some so bad I don't know where the scar ends and his face begins.

"N-Nova help," I stutter, still unable to look away from the ugly Constable.

Nova looks up and sees the Constable. His eyes go wide. He stands up, the door completely uncovered now. Suddenly, Nova knocks the staff out of the Constable's hand, then picks it up and points it at the Constable, who still grips my arm tightly. He moved so smoothly it looked like he'd done it a thousand times. I was not expecting that.

"Drop the staff," Nova growls, his lips twitching as he stares at the Constable with disgust.

"Y-you better do what he says," I stutter to the Constable.

"You have no business being near her," Nova continues.

The Constable huffs, clearly mad. He seems to know something I don't and shoves me toward Nova without a word, slowly backing away.

"Open the door and go down. I'll be right behind you," Nova instructs.

I open the trapdoor and drop down. I hear a few grunts of pain, and some loud thumps. Then Nova drops down behind me still holding the staff he had taken from the Constable. He rolls his shoulders, trying to calm down after whatever he did.

Chapter Five

Ara

"Nova, are you okay?" I ask as I turn to him after we had walked a little way down the passage.

He still grips the staff tightly, like he was holding onto it for dear life. His silvery eyes flick from one spot to the next. I study his face, bright silver eyes, a soft, rounded nose, pale turquoise lips, and dark brown hair hanging in his face. He lets out a puff of air, blowing wisps of hair out of his eyes.

"The real question is, are you okay?" he asks coming over to me. He looks me over, grabbing my chin and turning my face to both sides so he could examine it for cuts or bruises.

"Nova, I'm fine." I sigh as I gently push his hand away. I stare at his face again, this time I notice a slash across his right cheek and purple blood seeping out.

"Nova," I exclaim, "You're hurt." I reach up and brush my thumb across his cheek, noticing other scars as I did so. Scars I couldn't see, but could feel. They matched the size and shape of some of the scars the Constable had.

"It's nothing. I'll be fine," he grunts and turns away from me.

"Stop acting like that and being so stubborn. It's not nothing. Now come here so I can have a look," I beg. "You don't have to act all fierce and overprotective. There is no one else down here for you to scare into leaving me alone."

He sighs and turns back toward me, knowing I wasn't going to give up until I was able to have good look at the cut. I look at the gash along his cheek then I pull my pack off my back. I dig for the regeneration kit. I quickly open it and pull out a clean, sterilized cloth.

"Here," I say quietly as I dab away the blood. I wipe the dripping blood from his cheek before it has a chance to stain the crisp white shirt of his Tan Dew.

"Ara, I should be the one taking care of you. Those Constables were after hybrids. They were after you," Nova says softly as he pushes my hand down.

"Yes, but you were there..." I trail off as I think. "Nova, how did you defeat him? I have never heard any stories of a normal Human, Oderian or hybrid defeating a Constable. I know for a fact the only other people who could possibly stand a chance against a Constable is another Constable."

"Ara, there is a lot you don't know about me. Your father warned me a long time ago about something like this happening. The Council's whole plot has been in the works for moons. I..." he faltered, not wanting to continue.

"How did my father know you could keep me safe? How did you beat the Constable?" I choked, slowly starting to see where this was going and not liking it.

"At one point I was a Constable. I was forced to train. I was forced to hurt innocent people, Ara. Your father knows. He knows I am the one person on this entire planet who could even try to keep you safe. It's a good thing, actually, that the Council is starting a war because if the Council doesn't exist then the Constables don't exist either," Nova bellows, suddenly breaking his calm demeanor. "I know what you think about them. I know you think they are monsters, and...they are. But that's not me. That isn't who I am, you should know that. I hated it. I hated hurting people."

I stare at him. I never knew he was a Constable. I could never imagine him as one. He is the calmest, and most un-constable like person I know. How could my father have known when I didn't? Why did he never tell me? Why would my father even trust my life in the hands of a Constable? "That's why you were able to fight a Constable and live," I conclude softly.

He nods as he breathes in deeply, trying to calm himself down. "Yes."

Suddenly, we hear footsteps coming down the passage. It sounds like boots.

I stare at Nova, my eyes wide. I guess the Constables followed us down here. It's happening again, and this time we are trapped. No secret trap doors to escape down, either we stay and fight or we run and hope the Constables don't catch up.

"Stay behind me," Nova says, as he turns toward the direction the sound is coming from. "If I tell you to run, then you turn. Once you do, run as fast as you can," Nova instructs, seeming to take the first choice and the second as a failsafe.

"Okay," I reply as the sound comes closer and closer. It echoes off the walls of the passage making it sound as if there were hundreds of Constables coming down the hall to take us to our doom. I know if they catch us, they will probably kill us both and make examples out of us, showing the rest of Ode exactly what they would do to those who ran.

My head continues to spin as we stand there waiting. Maybe I should run, how do I know Nova is going to protect me? For all I know, he could be working with them to get me. Maybe this was all part of some crazy plan the Council came up with? Constables don't change. They will never change. They are cruel and violent by nature.

Seconds later the Constables come into view and I see five. I sigh in relief, five, not hundreds. My eyes move from the Constables and land on Nova. He grips the staff, his knuckles turning white. His body is tense with a grim expression set on his face.

"If it isn't Nova Stargazer himself." The Constable in the front laughs as he leans on his staff. "Who's the pretty hybrid behind you?"

"You aren't going to touch her," Nova growls.

When Nova gets mad, it's almost like he is a completely different person, someone who is relentless and rarely has any mercy...like the rest of the Constables. I see it now, how could I have been so blind? Maybe he is a monster like the rest of them.

"It looks like someone isn't having a great day. I have news. Your day isn't going to be getting any better." The Constable smiles wickedly, he leans over slightly to have a better look at me and says, "Did you know Nova was one of the best Constables we have ever had? Did you know how he has killed too many innocent people to count? He knows there is a price tag on your pretty little head and the one reason why he is protecting you is so he can turn you in for the money."

My hearts leap into my throat, and my eyes widen. My suspicions may be true. I turn to Nova, "Is he correct?"

He shakes his head. "No, don't listen to them Ara, they are lying to you. I told you, your father asked me to protect you. I would never betray you or your father."

"The Council said that to my father too. Look how that turned out," I mumble.

"Come on little hybrid, do you believe him? Come with us and we'll keep you safe from people like him." The Constable grins slyly.

His grin scares me, even more than Nova does at the moment. I shake my head. I think I would rather take my chances with backstabbing and lying Nova, than with those wicked Constables. Nova keeps the staff pointed at the Constable who had been talking. They form a circle around us and point the tips of their staves at Nova and me.

"N-Nova, do something," I whisper as I stare at the sharp point that is way too close for comfort. Here is the moment of truth. Will he really protect me? If he doesn't, I have no way to defend myself.

Suddenly, the Constables come forward, and Nova goes after the closest one, but two of them grab him from behind and two more grab me. I struggle to push them away, but they grip my arms tighter. They are trained to catch people and bend them to their will. I, however, am not trained to fend them off.

Nova struggles against the two holding him back. The Constable who had been talking earlier walks over to me and snatches my chin, forcing me to look at him.

"You are such a pretty hybrid. It will be a shame to see you go, but yet that price, it is so much better." He frowns slightly at me.

"Why would the Council want me? I've never done anything to

anger them," I ask as I turn my head, pulling it out of his hand.

"You are one of the last hybrids still free. You are also the daughter of a former Council member. The Council can't have any loose ends hanging around. They have the world to take over, and an entire race to erase from the universe. The Council wants you dead, so they have arranged an award for the Constables who catch you, then you get to be executed," he explains joyously as he grabs my face again.

"Get your grimy paws off her," Nova growls as he struggles against his two captors.

"We need to get you to the Council and the easiest way to get you there is if you aren't awake and causing a scene. I would hate to have to kill you before the Council sees your pretty little head alive. The rest of the Constables would miss out on such a wonderful execution. So, I will use this magnificent device. It won't hurt, I promise...to tell you the truth I don't really know," the Constable says, smirking, as he pulls out a small silver cylinder.

I have a feeling I really don't want to know what is inside it. I glance over at Nova. He is still struggling, but can't seem to escape the grips of the Constables either.

"No," Nova exclaims when he sees the silver cylinder, seeming to know exactly what is inside the device. "You can't inject her with that. It has killed more people than are in the Constable force. You should know that of all people here. I know your family died thanks to its testing because so few survived it. I don't know how it was put into use."

"It was all for the sake of the Council. Besides my family are the Constables in my force. I would never betray them...Unlike you Stargazer," the Constable sneers. "And death, the hybrid could die, but it is a risk we will have to take." The Constable shrugs.

The rate of my three hearts speed up as the Constable presses the cylinder to my neck. I can feel myself shaking, and I can't stop it. I hear a click. Suddenly there is a searing pain in my neck. The two Constables who were holding me push me forward. I hold my neck and let out a wail as I stumble. I get my footing for a moment.

"Nova?" I ask softly not able to focus my eyes, or my brain. *What am I doing letting him watch me pass out? What if he is still working with the Constables? Right now, he is the one person I can somewhat trust. Maybe I should ask him to stay with me?*

I start to see gray spots. They slowly take over my vision, until I can't see anything.

"Yes, I'm right here," I hear Nova whisper, he seems to be right next to me, but I can't see him.

"D-don't leave me here," I stutter, my hearing starting to fade out.

"Never planned on it," he replies, this time sounding far away.

Suddenly, I can't even hear anything. I feel my legs crumple underneath me, and I hit the ground.

Chapter Six

Nova

I finally find the strength to pull myself from the Constables' grasp as Ara crumples to the ground. I snatch up her limp hand, checking for her pulse. I glance at her face, watching for the silver tears Oderians cry when they die. The silver will leak out of our eyes in tears. This lets people know we are dead.

I sigh in relief when I don't see any, and her pulse, though a little slow because two of her three hearts are beating, is steady.

"See she's fine. The stuff stops one heart and leaves the other two beating," the Constable exclaims.

"It's still going to affect her body. If something were to happen to her in this state, one of the two hearts that are beating right now will stop and we all know what happens then," I say as I stand up facing the leader of the small group of Constables.

"Then she will die. It's a better way to go than how she will once we take her," he sneers as he walks over and leans into my face, "Believe me, it's much less painful."

"You aren't going to lay another finger on her or else I swear the silver will be running rivers out of your eyes," I growl at him as I point my staff at his chest.

He leans in further over Ara, sets his boot on her stomach and whispers harshly, "Try me. I will take her from you and to the Council."

I automatically turn the staff to the blunt end and slam it into his chest, sending him stumbling backward. "Over my dead body," I sneer.

Once he regains his balance, he runs at me with the sharp

tip of broken glass from the globe on his staff, pointed straight at my head.

I jump over Ara, so she is now behind me. I bring up my staff and block the attack, diverting his momentum away from me, and he goes stumbling off again.

He turns back around and smiles, "So, Nova Stargazer the stories they tell about you are true. You really have no weakness..." He pauses, staring at me intently, "But one meager little hybrid girl. Wouldn't it be terrible if she died even though you pledged to lay down your life to protect hers?"

I whip around to Ara and find one of the Constables, which I had completely forgotten about, holding his staff above her, ready to plunge it through one of the two beating hearts she has left.

"No," I exclaim.

Due to the distraction, I am suddenly yanked back and held there by another Constable while one keeps their staff pointed at Ara, and the leader walks around me, frowning.

"I don't understand your attachment to this hybrid. Nova Stargazer, you are a full blood Oderian, why are you keeping her safe? You can turn her in and get the reward, then find yourself a nice full blood Oderian girl and settle down," he says as he stands in front of me. "Why do you protect her?"

"It doesn't matter why, as long as I don't fail her," I say calmly, as I keep my eyes on Ara.

"There is something more. More than the connection two already have, you are what, two hundred forty moons old and she is two hundred twenty-eight, there could be something there." The Constable grins as he talks.

My hearts start beating faster because he hit it right on the mark. There is something more I feel for her, more than the relationship we have now. I can't say anything, though. It would put Ara in more danger than she is already.

"Ha," the Constable exclaims. "I knew it. I can see it in your eyes." He takes several steps closer. "Admit it. Admit that Nova Stargazer has fallen in love with a hybrid girl. Oh my. The Council is going to eat this up. You will be the talk of the Council and Constables for moons."

I frown at him, Ara should never find out about this, this could change her whole life, how she sees me. Then again, I've already screwed up her image of me by revealing I was a Constable. There is no going back now.

"You know I'm right, Nova. How could you stoop so low and let this happen? What if the Council never started this and she had fallen in love with you, too? What would the rest of Ode thought had they found out? Nova, what would have happened?" With each question, he steps closer and closer until he stands right in front of me.

"I don't know," I exclaim, breaking my calm demeanor once again today. "I don't know what would have happened but it sure as hell would have been better than what is about to happen to you."

I rip my arms out of the Constable's grasp and pick up my staff in one swift movement. I turn, knocking the end into the face of the Constable who was hovering over Ara. He goes stumbling back and hits the wall with a thud, then slides down it holding his face and groaning in pain.

"There is a reason why they say I am the greatest Constable that will ever exist. I realized how wrong the rest of you all were. There should be peace and the Council needs to see that. Ara's father couldn't do it, so I intend to make them," I say, as I stand. "And a few Constables like you are not going to get in my way, so move or I will kill you," I growl.

"So, you still have your fierceness. Haven't quite gone soft yet, Stargazer?" the Constable laughs.

"I have no feelings, you should know of all people. I killed a number of your Constable family while I was training. I will not blink twice now," I reply.

"If you feel nothing then you will feel no guilt when we kill her. The Council doesn't care if we bring her to them dead or alive," he says, raising his staff and pointing it at Ara.

I run at him, my staff raised, aimed for his chest. He blocks my staff with his own, then thrusts its sharp edge at me. I deflect it and wheel around him, faster than he could even blink. I position myself behind him. Before he could turn, I slam my staff into the back of his legs. He falls to his knees. I turn my staff to the blunt side, hitting him square in the back. He sails forward and lands face first in the dust with a loud "oomph". Next, I smack the staff into the side of his head and knock him out.

I flip my staff to the end with the sharp globe and thrust my staff down, through his back and his cuirass, until I feel it hit the stone floor of the passage. Blood spurts everywhere, dripping down my cuirass and staining my crisp white shirt with its purple hue.

I look up to see the other three Constables staring at me in fear.

"Get out of here before you end up like him," I snap, motioning to the dead Constable on the ground, who lies in an ever-growing pool of his own blood.

They quickly turn and run away, back the way they came. I let out a sigh, trying to calm the racing of my hearts. I shake out the tenseness in my arms and flex my fingers, trying to get feeling to return to them.

As I turn, I slide my stolen staff into a holder on my back from when I was a Constable. I figured it might come in handy to have.

I kneel down and take Ara's wrist once again, checking her pulse. Two hearts still beat, so I gently pick her up and cradle her in my arms and continue on our way down the dimly lit passageway to safety. The blood on my cuirass soaks through Ara's cloak, but I don't have time to worry about cleaning it up at the moment. I have to get us out of here and as far away from those Constables and the Council as I can.

I can't believe I told her I was a Constable and how her father knew long before she ever did. She will never trust me again. I understand why she thinks they are monsters. They really are, but she knows me. She knows I would never hurt her. I mean, I love her, but she can't ever know. It hurts that it has to be this way but, the Constables know, and now they are desperately going to try to use us against each other. She knows I am a cold-blooded killer, which is hard enough for her to handle right now.

I glance down at Ara. She looks so peaceful, so beautiful. I shake my head. *No, Nova, you are not allowed to think like that.* I shift her slightly in my arms, her head rests against my chest now, her legs still hang limply, bent at the knees over my arm.

I look back up to watch where I am going. I see where the tunnel ends. We still have a long way to go before we get to safety.

Chapter Seven

Nova

I walk out of the cave, still holding Ara in my arms. I squint as my eyes adjust to the light. Looking around, I see we are in a valley in between two mountains. There are very few mountains on Ode, and the ones that do exist have not been thoroughly explored. They would be the perfect places for rebel bases to be hidden safely. I carefully walk toward an older Oderian who sits on a rock, wrapped tightly in his cloak. He looks out of place in the barren landscape. He must work with the rebels.

"State your name and business," he says gruffly.

"Nova Stargazer. I'm traveling to the rebel base in need of shelter and to join in the rebellion," I decree. He looks at me closely, probably noticing the dried blood on my cuirass.

He motions to Ara still limp in my arms, "Who is she?"

"My friend, she's gone into regenerative shock. We need to get to the base as fast as possible," I urge.

He nods his head, "Follow me."

I follow him through the valley to a fairly secluded spot. We stop next to a small H.P.V., a hydro-powered vehicle.

The engine of the vehicle comes to life. A small bit of a liquid drips from the bottom of the vehicle.

"Don't touch it. You should know these things run off Takaw. You should also know how corrosive it is. If you would like to keep your skin, don't go near it," the man says.

"Where did you get the H.P.V.?" I ask. "I thought only Constables and the Council had those."

I have to act like I don't know how easy it actually is to steal one. Then again, that is something the Council and Constables know.

Sometimes I hate acting like a normal Oderian.

"The rebels stole quite a few of them and now use them for transportation," he explains.

It has a sleek design, and is about as long as two of my arm spans in length. The Oderian knocks on the back and it opens to reveal another Oderian, who motions for us to get in. I think I can safely assume he is the pilot.

"Is she in regenerative shock?" asks the Oderian from inside the H.P.V.

I nod as I stand there awkwardly, still holding Ara in my arms.

"Set her down on the floor and we will get going. Oh, and give her a shot of this, it will help get her heart started again without a regeneration tube," he says holding out a small vial as I carefully set Ara down. I take the vial and he then disappears into the front of the ship to, I assume, take off.

I feel the H.P.V. rumble beneath me and lift into the air. I glance at Ara and kneel down next to her. Should I give her the stuff the rebel gave me? I roll the vial between my fingers, contemplating this. Can I trust them with her life? I know they can be tricky but, I don't think they would kill an innocent hybrid like the Council is willing to do. Besides, the rebels were formed to oppose the hybrid genocide, not to help the Council enact it. Carefully, I lift her head up and set it in my lap. I brush a few stray wisps of hair from her face. I press the vial to the side of her neck and click the button. It lets out a hiss, and it injects the fluid into her bloodstream.

"Be careful when she wakes up," the older Oderian says, "If she gets too worked up then she will go into regenerative shock again."

I nod and look back down at her. I have to keep her safe through this, even if she hates me for it, I can't risk her being killed. They would have to kill me first. I promised her father I would do this...I promised myself I would do this.

Her eyes shoot open and focus on me. A small smile forms on her face but it quickly disappears.

"Ara, are you alright?" I ask.

Suddenly she jumps up, backing away from me. I see a glint of panic in her eyes, her chest heaves as her eyes flick from place to place, slowly taking in her surroundings before landing back on me.

I stand up and slowly walk toward her, "Are you okay?"

"S-stay back," she stutters as she backs away from me.

"It's me Ara. I'm not going to hurt you," I say softly as I take another step toward her.

She shakes her head as she backs further away from me. "No, you are covered in blood." She glances down at herself, "I'm covered in blood..."

"Ara," I try again, "It's okay, and it's not your blood. I would never hurt you."

"You killed someone, though. You're a Constable, and they are all the same. You're going to take me to the Council and have me executed," she panics.

"No, I won't. I'm not a Constable anymore, you know that," I whisper as I take a few more steps towards her.

She continues to back away and backs right into the wall of the H.P.V. "Please, stay back," she begs as she holds out her arm as if to keep me from getting any closer.

I continue to step closer to her; I reach out and softly take her hand.

"Let go of me!" she exclaims as she tries to pull her hand out of mine. I let go of her hand and take another step toward her.

I gently set my hands on her shoulders. I can feel her trembling with fear and the glint of panic from earlier returns to her eyes.

"Let go of me you monster," she cries as she tries to pry my hands off her shoulders. When she fails she starts to beat on my chest.

"Let go." She pushes me, but I don't move. "Please. Let go."

Suddenly, her eyes roll back into her head and she collapses into my arms. I turn around with her slumped against me and slowly slide down the wall as I lower her to the floor.

I can feel my hearts breaking as I pull her up against me. Her head rests in the crook of my neck, and I wrap my arms around her as I bury my face in her shoulder.

She hates me. She's afraid of me. She's afraid I will hurt her. She thinks I am a monster. All because she knows I was a Constable. All because I vowed to protect her, even if it meant killing like I used to.

"I'm sorry Ara. I'm so sorry," I mutter as I grip her tighter. "It shouldn't be this way, but I promise I will keep you safe. I promise I will never hurt you."

"It's not your fault. Most of what she said was the regenerative shock trying to wear off. She was too worked up. It happens all the time. Give her time to heal, she should be alright with a little care," says the older Oderian.

I look up at him, "It is my fault. She shouldn't be stuck in the middle of this because, inevitably, she is going to get hurt and it's going to be my fault."

"Then you protect her and earn her trust back."

He shrugs like he understands the situation I'm in. I don't think he does, though, this entire situation is complicated beyond belief and I have no idea how I'm going to get Ara and myself out of the mess I created.

I sigh, "I'm going to try no matter what. I'm worried I will never be able to earn it back completely." I glance down at her, I hate Constables. This is what they do. They turn people against each other...They turned her against me.

I slam my head back against the wall of the H.P.V. *Why did I ever think it was a good idea to become a Constable?*

Suddenly I feel the H.P.V. hit the ground, I guess we made it.

The Oderian stands as the pilot comes back in and opens the door to let us out. I lift up Ara again and carry her out of the H.P.V., I gasp as I glance around, the base is huge. Much bigger than the small group of buildings I imagined. A large building is set atop a slight hill and it overlooks a small cluster of houses that, I assume, accommodate the majority of the rebel force.

"Follow me," the older Oderian says as he starts to walk to the larger building. "Our commander wants to see you."

I follow hesitantly. I hope the rebels will allow us to join, but it is a little dangerous for them to take everyone they pick up straight to their commander. I pause for a second to think, the Constable in me bringing more of my suspicions to the surface. It is possible they do know about my past, about my time as a Constable. If they know, it could pose a few...more than a few rather large problems.

I am lead to the large building, then shown to a practically empty room. There was nothing inside, no chairs, no nothing, but there was another door at the end of the room.

I carefully set Ara down on the floor, leaning her against one of the perimeter walls. I wonder what is going on here.

The door on the far side opens and someone enters, it's too dark for me to make out any facial features. All I can see is the silhouette of a body. It looks to be slightly stocky but muscular. However, the cloak may distort the silhouette slightly.

"Who are you?" A deep voice booms.

"My name is Nova Stargazer," I say confidently. Hopefully, my reputation does not precede me, I must play this out. Act innocent and maybe they will buy it.

"And why have you come here?" the voice asks.

"My friend and I have come here wanting to join the rebels and in search of shelter from the Council," I respond, trying to sound confident in my story.

"I see. I have heard of the name Nova Stargazer."

"What exactly have you heard?" I ask. I was really hoping it wouldn't come to this. This may not be good for Ara and me.

"I have heard how you were a ruthless Constable. Why do you help the hybrid?"

I pale, it's a good thing it is dark enough in here that he can't see me, my face would give everything away. "I am no longer a Constable. I disagree greatly with what they are doing. I want to keep my friend safe."

"Interesting. How do I know you are not still working with them and this is all a ruse to infiltrate our ranks?" the voice asks, slightly intrigued.

"Ask my friend, she is one of the last hybrids still free," I state.

"We will. To be certain, we will have to detain you until we have decided if you are truly here for the reason you say."

"But…"

"No. It is final." The man finishes and leaves the room through the same door. I turn around and see two Oderians picking up Ara.

"No. What are you doing?" I exclaim as I run over.

"We need to take her for questioning, as our leader stated before," one says.

"No, you can't. She's in regenerative shock." I state harshly.

They can't take her without me being there when they question her. She still thinks I am a Constable.

"You need to calm down. You cannot go with her for reasons beyond our control. I will take you somewhere else," the other says.

"No." I try to go after the one carrying her but the other holds me back. "Let go of me." I exclaim. The Oderian twists my arms behind my back and I am unable to move them. Even some positions are impossible for a former Constable to escape from.

The other rebel holds her as I had earlier, her head resting against his chest. My anger flares as I continue to struggle. I have to get to her. The Oderian keeps walking ignoring my protests. He carries her to the same door I entered from.

Then the door closes and she is gone. "Damn it," I yell after them as I struggle to break free.

"Let's go," the Oderian says from behind me. He pushes me to the other door which was left open.

"Where are you taking me?" I ask harshly as I continue to struggle.

"To a cell. You have been too violent for us to allow you to be free until we know for sure you are not a Constable and working with the Council," he says.

I groan. This is not working out the way I want it to.

Moments later I am sitting in a small cell. The door is locked, and the one view of the outside world I have is a small window in the door. I have a feeling that I may be here for a while.

A feeling of uneasiness washes over me, Ara is going to tell them about her suspicions. While most of them are true, I am not going to kill her. I am also not a spy for the Council. The rebels don't know enough about me to know I would never betray Ara, even if it meant my life was at stake.

Ara knows, though. She is smart enough. She should be able to figure everything out eventually. It may take some time, but I have faith in her. She knows she is the last chance I have.

Chapter Eight

Ara

I groan as I wake up. My head pounds with every beat of my hearts. Slowly, I open my eyes. Everything seems to be blurry at first, but then it clears up.

Glancing around, I see I am in a regeneration tube in a small room, sadly not mine, and not at home. I was really wishing everything that happened was a dream and I would wake up in my regeneration tube with Nova there and I would be able to trust him.

Where is Nova? In fact, where am I?

I push open the regeneration tube and something starts beeping loudly. *What is going on?* I start to sit up but a wave of dizziness washes over me. I close my eyes for a second to let it pass. I open my eyes again, taking a deep breath. Suddenly the door opens and a human walks in.

"Good to see you are up," he nods in my direction.

"Who are you?" I ask tentatively. For all I know I could be in the Council's custody because Nova had been lying to me. I take a good look at the man. He is much older than me.

"I am the leader of the rebels." The man responds with a smile, his teeth are crooked and out of place. The scars on his face wrinkle up oddly when he smiles.

"Where is the Oderian I came here with?" I ask. Maybe the rebels know if he is really working with the Council.

"We have him in custody," he answers.

"Why?" This might be good. They may have more information on him.

"He was too violent to be let loose around the base. We also

40

have some questions to ask you before we allow you or him to be released," he says, sitting down in a chair on the other side of the room.

I shrug, "Alright. Please, ask what you need to."

"We already know you are a hybrid. How long have you known Nova?" he asks.

"For as long as I can remember."

"Did you know he was a Constable during some of time you have known him?" The man leans over and rests his elbows on his knees.

"I do now. I found out not too long ago. He claims he isn't one anymore, but I-I don't know. With what is going on right now I don't know who I should trust and who I shouldn't. I honestly don't know what to believe. I've heard stories, horrible stories about how some try to leave the Constables but they never truly can," I reply as I glance down at my hands set in my lap.

He nods. "Understandable. That is all we wanted to hear. If you do not trust him, then we will not either. We will find out if he is truly still working for the Constables," he says. "We will come and get you when we know he is not a threat."

"Thank you," I say as he leaves.

"I will be right back. I can give you a tour of the base if you like?" he asks.

"I would like that," I answer.

He leaves the room for a moment, to tell someone what he found out, I assume.

As sinking feeling settles itself in my stomach, I feel bad for saying those things about Nova. I shake my head, no. I shouldn't feel bad about saying those things. He is the one who lied to me all these moons and kept something as big as being a Constable from me.

The rebel leader came back in moments later. "Now, let me show you around so when you leave this room you won't get lost and unable to find your way back."

I follow him back out the door of my room and into the hallway. I glance up and down, not seeing another person.

"Most of us rebels are training. We must be ready for whatever the Council decides to throw at us. I welcome you to our base, hybrid. You will be safe here," he tells me. "Now, if you went straight down this hallway you would hit a dead end." He points to one side, "If you want to go anywhere, you must go the other way." He points the opposite direction and starts walking.

I follow him down the hall, trying to memorize the way in case I was in need of anything, like getting out of here quickly if things get out of hand.

"Food is served in there." He points at a closed door as we round the corner.

We pass by two doors that lead outside the base. I mentally note their position for future use.

"We train in there," he says as I peek through the window in the door and see more people than I can count all training and working on their fighting skills. "We need plenty of practice if we will ever defeat the Council and the Constables."

I follow him back to my room, "That is all you need to see for now. I will go check to see if we have gotten any information from your companion yet."

He leaves me alone once again, and I kick myself for not catching his name. I should know it. He is the leader of the rebels after all.

I sit down, slowly starting to process what happened. Why must I be alone during such a stressful time as this? Sighing, I close my eyes and images of Nova fighting those Constables haunt my mind.

I shouldn't be thinking about him, or anything that has to do with him. I need to figure out how I am going to survive this war. I could stick with the rebels. It's likely they will keep me safe because I am a hybrid.

Nova would know what to do...I stop myself before I finish the thought. It doesn't matter what Nova would do, he is locked up away from me because he is a Constable. *The question is, what would Ara do? What would I do?*

I pace the room, my mind reeling with the many decisions I need to make. There was a point in time where I would have trusted him with my life, but now I'm not so sure. I am the one person here who can free him.

Maybe I need more time to think.

A sudden knock on the door startles me out of my thoughts. The rebel leader left a few moments ago. It's unlikely he could be back already. I know no one here. Why would anyone want to talk to me?

"Come in?" I call but it comes out as more of a question.

The door slides open, and a girl stands in the doorway, holding what I think is a fresh, clean shirt folded up. She looks to be a little bit younger than me.

"Hello." She grins.

"Hi..." I trail off, this is strange.

"I heard there was a hybrid so I knew I had to come and see you." She walks in and leans against the wall, looking me up and down. "Plus, the big man himself asked me to bring you a fresh Tan Dew, seeing as how," she motions to my shirt, "Your's is currently covered in blood."

"You are seeing me." I sit down awkwardly on the regeneration tube. She hands me the clothes, then turns around, waiting for me to change.

"So, do you know whose blood it is?" she asks as I slip off my cloak followed by my cuirass.

"I'm not really sure. I think it belongs to a Constable. I don't know how it got on me," I reply as I slip off the bloody shirt and put on the clean one. I start to lace my cuirass back up. The girl turns back around.

"I'm a hybrid too you know." She changes the subject, standing up straight and coming toward me. "For the longest time I thought I was going to be the last of my kind, but not anymore. There are two of us now."

"Really?" I ask.

I thought I was the last free hybrid, that's why the Constables and the Council wanted me so bad. I guess it turns out I'm wrong.

"I'm Pandra," she says.

"Reminds me of Pandora, like the Greek myth," I state.

She tilts her head, confused. "I don't know what that is, but okay. What's your name?"

"Ara," I respond.

Pandra nods, "So you came in with a Constable?"

"Word travels fast here doesn't it?" I shrug trying to avoid the question.

I sit back down on the edge of the regeneration tube. I don't want to even think about Nova right now.

"It does when it has to do with a hybrid coming into the base with a Constable," she exclaims.

She acts like this is the most interesting thing to happen here in a while. I know she is trying to pry for information, though. She's digging into a mess she does not want to get involved in, whatever she thinks it is. I think for a moment. Maybe they sent her in because she is a hybrid. Maybe they think I will tell her more because I will be comfortable. Interesting tactic.

"What was it like? Being so close to one and not even knowing?" she asks.

"I don't even know for sure if he is actually working for the Constables so I can't really answer the question." I turn away from her.

This is not helping my nerves and proceeding to make me more uncomfortable.

"Hmm, so you know him plenty about him then?" she pokes, continuing to try and pry information out of me.

"I do actually, so please stop asking." I frown as I turn back to her.

Pandra nods. "I find Constables fascinating. They say one thing but mean another. They are so quick to snap when you start pushing their buttons." She laughs joyously, like messing with Constables is the most fun she will ever have. "I love learning about their inner workings, the way they tick. I want to get inside their head so I will know how to tear them apart later on."

"Trust me when I say this, you will get nothing out of him. He is stubborn. He will fight until the last breath leaves his body," I sigh.

These rebels have a rude surprise heading their way if they get on the wrong side of Nova. It is likely someone will get hurt, and it will not be Nova.

There is another knock on the door, and the rebel leader walks into the room. "Pandra," he acknowledges.

She grins, like the leader coming in is her cue to leave. "It was nice to meet you. I look forward to being able to talk to you more and becoming close friends."

I sigh in relief as she walks out the door. She was really starting to get on my nerves. I turn to the rebel leader.

"Would you like to see Nova?" he asks.

I nod. I think I am ready. I need to know what is truly going on.

Chapter Nine

Nova

I sit calmly in the cell. It's not the first time things like this have happened, and it probably won't be the last. Suddenly the door opens, and the same guard from earlier walks in.

"It seems the hybrid you brought does not trust you. Therefore, we cannot. If you are a Constable we need to know everything," the guard says.

I shrug. "I'm not a Constable anymore. I know nothing, and even if I was, I wouldn't tell you anything. You should know how difficult Constables are to crack. Wait until you try me."

"We'll see." The guard cracks his knuckles.

"Please, feel free to try to get information out of me. I have nothing to hide," I retort calmly. Let it come as it may. I will sit here and take it.

His fist slams into the side of my head. "Tell me why you came here," he demands.

"I already did," I respond.

His fist slams into my head again. "The real reason."

"That is the real reason."

He goes on for hours until I lean against the wall of the cell, nose bleeding, most likely broken and lip busted, hoping this was what Ara wanted. To make sure I wasn't going to turn on her. I know defending myself would make it look like I had something to hide and couldn't handle a beating for information. It makes me look weak. No, I let them beat me.

I let my nose bleed, not wiping away the blood. I hope she sees me like this. I hope she truly understands I am on her side.

The blood drips down the side of my face, adding more blood stains to my already stained shirt. I stare at the small window in the door. Maybe now she will trust me. The guard said he would bring her, to show her what he did. To prove I am who I say I am. He said no Constable would be able to withstand the beating he gave me. He speaks the truth, even though I was unlike any other Constable when I was one. I have nothing to hide.

Suddenly, her face appears in the small window, and her eyes widen as they meet mine. I hear her exclaim, "Let me in there."

"I thought you didn't trust him?" the guard asks, confused.

"Let me in," she yells at him, her face contorted in pain. She may not trust me, but she feels guilty.

The door opens, and I continue to sit there as she sits down next to me. I don't turn my head to look at her. It would hurt too much.

"What have I done?" she whispers to herself. "They could have killed him."

She must think I'm dazed and can't hear her.

"Nova, I'm sorry. This is crazy, I was panicking and scared. My whole world literally imploded on itself," she says softly.

I finally turn my head, enough to meet her gaze, not saying a word.

"I still don't know if I can fully trust you, but I know you have earned some back." She stares at me sadly. "Why didn't you defend yourself? I know you could have."

"I wanted to prove who I was and my purpose. To protect you," I rasp.

She sighs, taking the corner of her cloak and dabbing away the blood with it. "Did you have to get beat up for it?"

"If beating me was going to get you and the rebels to trust me," I respond.

"Then what's the plan?" Ara asks, "How are we going to free the hybrids?"

I laugh, wincing slightly as I do so. I honestly hadn't thought this far ahead yet.

"You don't have a plan, do you?" she sighs.

"No, no, I do. We stay here and train. You need to learn how to fight. If you want to go free then you need to learn how to protect yourself.

I won't be able to protect you from them forever. There will be a time when we will fight together," I tell her.

Hopefully, the Council won't get to me before then and force me to fight against her.

Chapter Ten

Ara

I lie in my new regeneration tube and stare at the ceiling of the small room I share with Nova.

What if we have a squad of troops go to the public execution and try to save the hybrids, humans, and Oderians who would otherwise die? Would the Constables outnumber us? Would any of us even make it out alive? How did the Constables even know a group of rebels was meeting there? Why does the Council want me so badly? What is so special about me?

"You alright Ara? You've been a bit out of it these past few days," Nova asks, startling me from my thoughts as he peeks over the side of the tube.

"I'm fine," I lie, still staring at the ceiling.

We've been staying at the rebel base for several days now, and these questions have run through my mind a thousand times. I still come up with no answer.

"Ara, I can tell you are lying," Nova sighs.

"You know me so well," I groan sarcastically as I sit up and perch on the edge of the tube.

Nova sits down next to me on the edge of the tube and looks at me expectantly. Sighing, I study the symbol of the rebels carved into the wall on the other side of the room. It is supposed to stand for freedom, for the freedom of hybrids.

I haven't felt very free, cooped up in this base, bored out of my mind for the past few days. Other than Nova trying to compensate for the fact that he lied to me for moons, I have had nothing to do.

I suddenly turn to him without thinking, and I say, "All of this is overwhelming, Nova. One minute everything is fine, the next we're running from Constables and staying in a rebel base. I find out I'm one of the last free hybrids and you expect me to be okay with that? Knowing all the people I have spent most of my life with are gone? It takes its toll on a person." I hold my head in my hands. "It's not as easy as you think."

What am I doing? I'm not supposed to confide in him. I still don't trust him like I used to.

Nova sighs, "You know, I have lost friends and family during this too. We have to look on the bright side of things and believe it will get better. I don't understand why the Council is doing this. I plan on finding out and stopping it, even if I die in the process."

I look over at him. "Look on the bright side of things? Says former Constable Doom and Gloom. Here, I'll kill someone and that will make me feel much better." I roll my eyes.

He frowns at me. Maybe I let myself go a little too far. I look down at my hands again, trying to avoid his eyes.

He puts his hand under my chin and lifts my head up, forcing me to look into his silver eyes. His face is set with a grim expression, "We have a plan to bring troops to the public execution and save as many people as we can. It's a long time from now, but we need to get ready. Knowing you, Ara, you won't want to sit here in in the safe base, and I'm not going to put you out there with a bunch of Constables unprepared, so we are going to go train."

He pulls me to my feet and out of the room.

I guess training is better than sitting around doing nothing. I need to get his words out of my head. They aren't true. His intentions are not what he says they are.

He leads me down the hall, suddenly coming to an abrupt stop. I slam into his back and stumble backward.

"Ara." A high-pitched squeal echoes down the hall.

I wince as I peek around Nova and see Pandra.

"Who are you?" Nova asks.

I guess he hasn't met Pandra yet.

"I am Pandra. I'm a hybrid and I'm friends with Ara," she answers.

"Oka…" Nova starts.

"Where are you heading?" Pandra asks.

"To train?" I say but it comes out as a question.

"Fun, come on." She takes my hand and starts skipping down the hall.

I glance back at Nova, who was still standing there in shock. He shakes his head, shrugs, and follows.

Pandra leads me to the large room I saw when the rebel leader showed me around the base. On one side is a line of practice dummies. The opposite wall is lined with staves and other weapons. The floor is padded, and the room is full of other rebels training.

"Do you have any experience in hand to hand combat?" she asks me as she walks over to the wall lined with staves.

I shake my head. Pandra pulls off two staves and tosses one to me. She immediately turns and takes a swing at me. I panic, dropping my staff and covering my head with my arms. I wait for the stinging pain, but it never comes.

I open my eyes and find that Nova has blocked Pandra's attack.

"What was that for?" she asks, pouting.

Nova pulls the staff from Pandra's hands and throws it to the floor. "What were you thinking? She has no training, she can't defend herself."

Pandra shrugs. "I was using the same method I was trained with."

"Being thrown into combat does not work for every student," Nova says.

"It's the one way she will be trained fast enough. There is no time to waste. We need more people out on the battlefield, hundreds are dying every day," Pandra argues.

"So, you think she is another soldier, look at yourself. You two are the last two hybrids known to be alive and free. Yes, you should fight, but the future of your race is hanging in the balance. Her training cannot be half-assed for the sake of time." Nova takes several steps toward her.

Pandra cowers slightly but quickly regains her courage. "Who are you to say such things?"

"I am an Ex-Constable. I was up for General. Do not try my

51

patience. You do not want to find out what will happen to you."
Nova takes another step forward, towering over Pandra.

"You don't scare me. I could take you on any day," she
laughs, she swings her leg and takes Nova's legs right out from
underneath him.

"Try me," Nova growls.

He snatches up the staff he took from her earlier. He swings,
but she ducks out of the way. Pandra, thinking quickly, takes the
staff she gave me.

Nova swings again. This time Pandra brings her staff up and
blocks it. Nova pushes, and Pandra goes stumbling backward. She
recovers quickly and pounces. Her offense is quick and separated
like she is trying to string together moves, but she can't come up
with them fast enough. Nova, however, moves fluidly. He links his
movements together but moves much faster than Pandra.

Soon Pandra's breaths come in short quick gasps. She is
getting tired. Nova continues on, not even fazed by the amount of
energy he is exerting to fight her.

I continue to watch as they fight, speechless and unable to
do anything. The other rebels who had been training stop to watch
the battle between Nova and Pandra. A circle forms around the two
as the battle goes back and forth.

Nova manages to hit Pandra on her side. She yelps in pain
and tries to connect her staff with any part of Nova's body, but she
can't.

Nova still doesn't let up on her. If he doesn't stop, I'm afraid
he might kill her.

"Nova," I call, "Nova, stop."

He doesn't seem to hear me.

Pandra tries another attack, swinging her staff around but
Nova blocks it, their staves knocking together. Nova shoves her
back, and she hits the ground.

The crowd gasps. He brings up his staff as if to deal the final
blow.

He is acting like a Constable. He probably can't control

himself. I take a step forward, slightly unsure of what to do, but I know I can't let him hurt her, or anyone else.

Without thinking, I place myself between them. "Nova, stop," I exclaim.

"Get out of the way," he growls, his eyes clouded over.

"No," I state. "Get back," I tell Pandra as I glance down at her.

"He might hurt you," she exclaims as she skitters away.

I shake my head, "He won't hurt me."

He growls, "Get. Out. Of. My. Way."

I take a breath. I can hear the thumping of my hearts in my ears. I carefully take the staff out of his hands and set it on the floor.

"Look at me," I whisper.

His eyes meet mine. They are still slightly clouded, but not as much as earlier. I set my hands on his shoulders, like he did to me on the H.P.V. when we were coming to the base. He doesn't shrink away like I did to him. His eyes start to wander away from mine.

"No, Nova look at me." I move my hands to his cheeks, cupping his face in the palms of my hands.

He eyes lock onto mine again. His breathing starts to slow back down to its normal pace. "I'm right here, don't worry about Pandra or anyone else. Only me." I run my thumbs along his cheekbone. I slowly trace the slash, now scar from the battle with the Constables before we came here.

He leans his head into my touch, his eyes lulling closed. Suddenly he wraps his arms around me, pulling me close. I lay my head on his chest. His three hearts slow down simultaneously, and beat at a slow steady pace. I slip my hands down and wrap them around his neck.

"Are you alright now?" I ask softly.

He sighs, "I think so." His voice rumbles in his chest. "I'm sorry."

I pull away from him, shaking my head, "I don't want to see you like that ever again. You were too much like a Constable. I hate to see you like that."

I glance around and find the crowd still watching us. I look down to my feet, slightly uncomfortable.

"I should go..." I trail off. I start to walk away but Nova catches my arm.

"Thank you," he breathes.

I nod, pulling my arm out of his grasp. I push through the crowd. I need to get away from everyone.

My mind starts to wander as I walk down the hall. *What did I do? Why did I let myself have a scene with Nova, in front of the entire base no less?*

I stop and lean against the wall of the hallway.

After everything that has happened the past few days, I had to go and have an intimate moment with someone I don't even trust. Someone I don't even know anymore.

I slide down the wall, holding my head in my hands.

I can still hear the beating of his hearts...Maybe that's my own. I honestly don't know. The feeling of his arms around me lingers, though. I can't say I didn't enjoy it, but I don't even know how I feel anymore.

As I sit there against the wall, my head continues to spin.

"Ara?"

I snap my head up at the sound of my name. I sigh when I see Nova.

"What are you doing out here?" he asks, sitting down next to me.

I shake my head, trying to avoid looking at him, "I needed some air."

"For some reason, I don't think that's true," he replies, suspicious.

"All those people, I..." I falter.

"You're embarrassed about what happened and that there were so many who saw it," he answers for me.

I nod, slightly surprised by how quickly he had figured it out.

"You still feel conflicted, though. You are angry about how I didn't tell you sooner, and you are mad at yourself for doing something you would have done before you knew the truth," Nova finishes.

"That's pretty much it," I mumble.

"I feel bad too, you know. I know I should have told you sooner, you probably wouldn't be as mad as you are now. I was afraid of how you would react. I did tell your father...He already knew because the Council knows everything. You didn't have to stop me. You could have let me kill her. That would have gotten rid of me. They would probably have me executed for killing a hybrid. Then you would really be the last one and you would never have to deal with me again." Nova pauses for a moment, like the idea of that scenario scares him. "But you didn't let that happen. Even if you are so angry at me you don't trust me anymore. You still could not bear to see me do something stupid and throw everything away."

I shrug, "I guess so."

"I was scared," he admits. "When she started coming toward you with that attack, I couldn't stop myself. I could never watch you get hurt without me having something to say about it. So...I jumped in.

"Thank you," I say, "I honestly didn't know what to do. You know I have absolutely no experience in that kind of thing. I can hardly say something rude to someone, let alone beat them up with a stick." I finally look over at him.

Nova smiles and nods, "I was the same way, but when push comes to shove and it's your life or someone you care for, in exchange for your opponent's life. You will choose the person you care about or your own every single time. No matter the situation."

"I-I don't know if I'm ready yet," I breathe.

"I can start teaching you as soon as you are. I'm in no rush and anyone who is can come speak to me about it." Nova puffs out his chest, trying to look big and strong.

I laugh, "You are too skinny for that to work, you know."

He grins, "It did exactly what it was supposed to do."

~ * ~

Thud. Thump. Thwack.

My staff keeps a steady pace as it continuously slams against the bag of dirt hanging from the ceiling.

55

Not long after my conversation with Nova, I decided I was ready. That was a moon ago, and all I have been doing since then is train.

"Hitting a target is easy," Nova says, watching from behind me, "The hard part is when it is trying to hit back."

I stop hitting the bag and turn to Nova. "How hard is it exactly?"

Nova picks up his own staff and smiles. "Try me."

I swing my staff to hit him in the chest. He blocks it and uses my own momentum to send me stumbling away. I flash back to the fight between Nova and Pandra. He tends to use the same defense but changes up his attacks.

I turn back around and aim at his arm this time. He blocks me once again, but this time instead of using my momentum against me, he advances. He controls his hits, never hitting me very hard. He taps lightly, but he moves at lightning speed, way too fast for me to even try to block or get in an attack. Then I take a step back and trip over my own feet. I end up sprawled out on my back with Nova's staff pointed at my chest.

My eyes look onto his, I half expect them to be clouded over, like after the fight with Pandra, but they aren't. They are as clear as they have ever been.

"Wow," I gasp, completely out of breath.

Nova lifts up his staff and stands up straight. "That's how hard it is," he replies.

He reaches his hand down, and I take it. He pulls me to my feet and takes my staff.

As he puts the staff away he says, "You did well. Maybe if you keep it up you will be as good as me."

I roll my eyes, so cocky. Over the last moon, I've started to see more and more of the qualities of a Constable in him. I go over the ever growing list of traits that I started. First his cockiness, plus he is definitely an egomaniac. He is overprotective, and he tends to be closed minded. Then again, he has always been like that. Nova isn't the type of Oderian to go around constantly speaking his mind. What he thinks usually stays closed off from the world.

Chapter Eleven

Ara

It's been several moons since we arrived at the base. They trust us, I guess. Nova and I have become two of the most useful agents that they have. They tend to send us out on missions, giving us barely enough time to recoup from the last one before sending us out on the next. Nova is getting sick of it because he has no time to train, so he has been getting hard to deal with.

I shake my head clear of those thoughts and try to focus on the issues at hand. We crawl slowly through the dust and dirt, no vegetation was in our way. We can't get caught. We are too far out from the base for them to send us back up, this is a do or be captured by Constables and executed by the Council kind of mission.

I glance over at Nova. His eyes are set on the small hideout that is our destination. I am still wary of him. I have found the Constables can be unpredictable. I'm never sure if he is truly on the rebel's side or not. One moment he is all in for the rebels, the next he isn't sure if he made the right decision about joining them. He should have felt that way about joining the Constables. He knew how I felt about Constables, so why did he join them? Did he have a sudden urge to kill or was there something more? Was there actually another reason why? He said he wanted to protect me. Did he really? I've been around him for almost my entire life, and I still can't come to understand how he ticks.

These last few moons I've been studying his actions and his emotions. He's very impulsive but most Constables are. He seems to want to protect me, watches out for me on missions but that could be him trying to get under my skin. Every positive trait I find, I end up twisting it until it looks like he is betraying me. I can't figure out what is really him or what my mind has made up anymore.

"Ara? Ara? Hello?" Nova calls in a whisper, pulling me out of my thoughts.

"What?" I respond, irritably.

"Did you hear what I said?" he asks.

"No," I sigh as I glance back at the hideout.

"You have to stop zoning out like that, it could get you killed," Nova scolds.

I roll my eyes, "Yeah I know."

He is always like this. I space out for a moment, I get a lecture about how, by coincidence, some Constable could sneak up behind me and slit my throat. What would Nova have to do then? He would have to kill them because he couldn't control himself, and no one would be there to stop him from killing every Constable on the planet during his temper tantrum.

I cringe, pulling myself out of his exaggerated scenario. That would never happen, and he knows it, because he would never let someone sneak up behind himself, let alone behind me.

"Anyway, we are going to split up. I'll take the front, and you take the back. Kill no one unless you have to. We want to get as much information as possible," Nova explains.

I glance away, rolling my eyes as I do so. He says 'kill no one' and he really means, 'I'll kill if I have too. You stay back and try not to let the blood spatter hit you.'

"Alright," I nod, looking back to him. "Extraction?"

"I will contact the base as soon as we have the information," he says. "Now, let's go."

I push myself up from the dirt and slowly make my way around the small base. There couldn't be more than maybe six Constables inside. Besides, Nova will have ended up taking care of them by the time I actually get in the hideout. Suddenly, I hear a crash from inside, so much for being covert. I slowly open the back door and creep in. At least it's Nova doing most of the dirty work, it's my job to actually gather the information and report it back at base. It's really a one-person job, but the rebels want Pandra and me out in the field. I guess so the rebels can rub in the Council's face that they still don't and will never have all the hybrids.

My eyes suddenly go wide, and my hearts seem to skip a beat. "No," I breathe as my eyes land on two dead hybrids. I kneel down to examine them. Bruises cover their arms and faces. They were beaten to death.

I swear one of these days I am going to end the Council. I carefully pull their cloaks off and drape them over the bodies since I do not have the shroud we would normally use. It is a ritual, and it represents the ages they died, though now that most hybrids are dead or in hiding, the cloaks will not be up to date.

I try to push the image out of my head as I walk through the door to the other room, holding my staff at ready, unsure if I will find more dead hybrids or their Constable murderers. I spot Nova on the other side of the room. He has two Constables sitting against the wall with his staff pointed at them. Ready to make the kill if necessary.

From the looks of the two, they have been here for a while. I guess the Council is short on Constables. If that is even possible. A small base like this would normally house six Constables. My mind immediately goes to the worst possible scenario it can come up with. *What if the other four Constables barge in while we are still here? Would Nova and I be able to escape? Would we have to stay and take our chances fighting?*

I shove those thoughts out of my head. We will deal with the Constables when and if we must. Right now, I have to focus on the task at hand.

I straighten up and walk toward the Constables. "Looks like we caught ourselves some murderers. What do you two have to say for yourselves?"

"Please don't kill us, show mercy," one exclaims as I pick at the top of my staff.

I roll my eyes. I never realized how wimpy Constables really are. When push comes to shove, they will break and talk. Unlike any other people on this planet, they will save themselves and no one else. They care for no one.

"You want mercy, hmm? Did you show mercy to those two dead hybrids? Did you? Or did you let them beg, pleading for their lives, giving them false hope until you bashed their heads in?" I sneer as I step closer to the Constable.

The Constable's eyes widen as he stares at me. I guess I really am scaring him. That's good. I don't usually scare Constables. Most of the time they cower in fear of Nova.

"Do you know what it feels like to have your head bashed in? It feels like your head suddenly starts to shrink, and it squeezes your brain. Blood will leak out of your eyes, nose, and mouth. The final blow cracks the skull and if it left a big enough dent, your brain will be leaking out of your ears," I exaggerate. I wonder how far I will be able to push until they want to run away screaming. The other Constable stares at me, his mouth hanging open.

"That's what you did to those two hybrids back there, and it's exactly what we will do to you if you do not tell us what the Council's plans are." I turn and walk to the other side of the room as I twirl my staff in my fingers. "So, what's it going to be?"

"Th-the Council was taken over, they have little say in what is done now. The leader, Zubenelgenubi, he has all the power. He stole the Council's plan and scaled it up. It's planet-wide now. He believes that humans and hybrids are ruining perfect Oderian lines. He has convinced the Council of this and now they want to end them. Most have been executed, but there is going to be one last execution in six moons. He told us to hunt down the last of the hybrids and bring them in or kill them on the spot. You were one he said to kill," one suddenly spills without a breath.

I glance at Nova and nod to him, indicating we are done here. As I leave I hear the thumps of the two Constables hitting the ground after Nova broke their necks.

As he catches up to me he asks, "Are you sure you're alright?" he asks, almost as if he didn't snap two Oderian's necks moments ago.

"Was it the fact I had to kill them? I told you to get the information we need. We cannot leave any survivors to speak out as witnesses against us. The Council can't know for sure where you are," he says, as I continue to walk.

"I don't care that you killed them. They deserved to die after what they did to those two hybrids. It's the fact there are few hybrids left on Ode, and to think I am one of the last is scary," I sigh.

Nova nods, turning away to contact base. He pulls out the tracker given to him before the mission. He presses the button for extraction. Seconds later he turns back around and says, "They should be here shortly."

I stand silently until the H.P.V. gets here, and we board it. I get comfortable in a seat, knowing I have a long ride back to base.

"Are you sure you are alright?" Nova asks after a few moments.

"I'm fine, I promise," I respond, leaning back against the seat and closing my eyes.

The H.P.V. falls silent again, all I hear are the sounds of my soft breaths and the occasional sigh from Nova. This will probably be all the silence I get for a while. The second we arrive back at base people will be rushing around, speaking to me, ordering me to go places.

The H.P.V. stays silent for a while. Suddenly there is a loud crash, and the H.P.V. trembles in the sky. My eyes shoot open. I look to Nova, who has jumped to his feet.

"What the hell was that?" he exclaims as he presses the button to open the door to the pilot.

The door slides open. The pilot presses buttons and flips switches one after another.

"Shots from the ground," the pilot answers flatly.

Nova groans, turning back to me. "One of them must have hit a panic button before I could take them both down. They alerted a bigger base and now they are tailing us, trying to shoot us down. Damn it."

He slams his fist into the wall of the H.P.V. making me jump.

"We have to do something before we get shot out of the sky. So, what are we going to do?" I stand, making my way over to

Nova.

I look out the front window of the H.P.V., nothing but flat land as far as my eyes can see. "Go faster," I say, "Let's see if we can outrun them."

"Those hydro-guns have a long range, Ara," Nova counters.

"What else can we do? Set this thing down and fight? That would be the worst idea you've ever had. We have no idea how many are down there. We have no idea exactly what weapons they have. We have no idea if they have back up. If you want to set down, by all means, take your chances. Personally, I would like to live to see tomorrow," I retort.

"What should I do?" the pilot asks.

"But..." Nova starts.

"Listen to me, Nova," I sigh.

"What do I do?" the pilot asks again.

Suddenly another blast hits the ship. I stumble into Nova as we both yell, "Go faster."

Nova hits the floor with a loud thump, groaning from my weight on top of him. I push myself up quickly, trying to avoid an awkward situation. I let out a puff of air, trying to blow a wisp of hair out of my face as I stand.

I straighten out my cuirass as I mumble, "Sorry."

Nova gets back up without a word and leans against the door frame, looking out the window.

"We seem to be losing them." the pilot states.

"Good," I nod, sitting back down.

The rest of the flight back to the base is calm. We land at the base. Nova and I don't exchange any words as we get off the H.P.V. I head straight back to my room, weaving through the masses of Humans and Oderians in the hallways of the base. I finally get back to my room and drop off my things. As I unload my pack I hear a light knock on the door.

"Come in," I drone. I hear the swish of the door opening and closing. I glance up and see Nova. "What do you want?"

"I came here to say that I am here if you want to talk," he says.

I burst into laughter, "Do you really think after everything you put me through I am going to come and confide in you? That's funny."

"Ara. I'm serious." He takes several steps closer, setting his hand on my shoulder.

I push his hand away. "Nova, I'm not the same hybrid I was when we got here. I was scared, helpless. I had no idea what was happening. Now? Now if you want to mess with me, make me mad, please, by all means, go ahead, but I'm going to warn you it's going to hurt. I'm tougher than I used to be. You really want me to confide in you? Then how's this, based on what those two Constables said, Father probably died all those moons ago because I didn't go back for him. I abandoned him. I abandoned him and everyone else I cared about. Guess what? I bet they are all dead now. Nova, I want to believe you, but I don't know if I can. I don't know if I ever will. So, you need to get over yourself and move on." I turn back to unloading my stuff.

I grab a cloth and my staff. I perch myself on the edge of my regeneration tube, and as I begin to polish my staff there is another knock on the door.

I sigh, "I can't catch a break, can I?" I close my eyes for a moment then open them and call, "Come in."

Nova looks at me as I glance up at the door to see who came in. I see that it is one of the main leaders of the rebels.

"Yes?" I ask as I turn toward him, putting on a fake smile.

"Messier would like to see you two," the Oderian says.

"Lead the way," I reply.

I slide my staff into the halter on my back as Nova and I follow him down the hall. The doors open to the main conference room, and we see the leader of the rebels sitting casually.

"Ahh, Nova, Ara, how nice of you to finally join us." He stands and comes toward us. He looks the same as he did the day I first came when he showed me around the base. He waves off the other man and his calm demeanor suddenly disappears. "We have very important matters to discuss, please sit." After motioning for us to sit down around a table, he leans back and props up his feet right in front of me. "What were you two able to find out on your mission?"

"Other than this Zubenelgenubi guy, nothing we didn't already know," I shrug as I sit down.

"Zubenelgenubi?" Messier asks.

"From what the Constable told us, he took over the Council, pretty much stole their plans and received credit for them," I explain, my eyes wandering around the room.

"Interesting," he nods. He turns to Nova. "Anything else?"

"We were ambushed on the way back, but we were able to lose them," Nova says.

"I should hope so, as you both know, the location of this base cannot be found out by any Constables, the Council, or this Zubenelgenubi. Many lives depend upon its secrecy," Messier warns.

I hum in agreement, picking at my cloak.

"Now, changing the topic, I have a new mission for you two. We are beginning to dwindle on supplies. Our supply line has been shut down, and our last shipment was intercepted by Constables. We cannot panic the people we are watching over. We need to get those supplies quickly before rations begin to get so small that people start noticing. There is no one else here with enough knowledge to be able to infiltrate a Constable base."

I nod as he continues to talk.

"Most of the time you would slip right in and slip right out. However, this time will have to be different. We will send you two in as captives. We will have several operatives already undercover waiting there to show you where to go and help our soldiers get back our supplies."

"Why can't your operatives do it?" Nova asks.

"If they were anywhere near the supplies the Constables would suspect something of them. We cannot risk exposing them. They provide too much valuable information to lose them. The mission must be done by you two, and it must be done quietly. If we make too much ruckus the Council will be able to figure us out. They will send backup to the base, and neither of you will be able to make it out alive," he explains.

I shrug, "Can't be that difficult."

Nova glares at me for a moment. "Are you sure about this Ara? We haven't even been back from our last mission for very long."

"What else am I going to do?" I continue to pick at my cloak.

"Alright," Nova sighs, turning back to Messier. "Where exactly is this base? Approximately how long will the mission take?"

"About that, there is more. We have several of our agents at the Constable base, and many others are being held there. We need you to help them escape, along with getting the supplies." Messier pushes a map over the table to us, and I study it. A path is drawn through the mountains, "You will follow that path on foot, and we don't have enough H.P.V.'s to spare one to take the two of you up to the pass. Once you have passed the mountains a group will meet you and take you to the base. Your extraction will be almost the same, you and the other prisoners you have freed will need to make it back over the mountains. Once over, a fleet of H.P.V.'s will meet you. There should be enough of you to carry back the supplies. I don't care how you get back to the mountains, but make sure you do."

"Are you sure this plan is secure?" Nova asks. "The Constables could easily kill all of us or even follow us back and massacre everyone on the base. That would spell the end for all rebel causes."

"There are lookouts stationed in the mountains. They will warn us if you are being pursued. Those lookout positions will also be your safe places along your route. A few of them are empty. You will be able to stay in those overnight on your way to the Constable base. Go and get prepared, your journey will start tomorrow," he finishes.

Nova and I stand, beginning to leave the room.

Nova leaves quickly, something obviously on his mind.

"Oh, and Ara," Messier says suddenly, before I exit the room. "Be easy on him, he is trying to make up for what he did. The least you can do is forgive him."

Chapter Twelve

In the Council Dwellings

Zubenelgenubi lounges casually on what he likes to think of as his throne. He nods to himself. He believes what he is doing for the people of Ode is good, it will cleanse them, he thinks, and revert them to their old ways.

It had taken him years to infiltrate the government with people who answer to him. He had to make sure when the time came for him to take over, the Council would be ready and the rest of Ode could do nothing about it. After all, there was no way for them to overthrow their own government without invoking a civil war.

A civil war was exactly what he wanted at the moment, though. He was sick of those pesky rebels hiding, waiting, and planning for the perfect moment to strike, especially with so many of his key players on that side.

"My Lord," someone interrupts him from his thoughts.

"What?" he growls as he stands from his 'throne' and stalks down toward the pure Oderian woman. He had thrown out any humans and hybrids that were still involved in the government.

"We have surveillance from one of the Constable hideouts. Two rebels broke in, then interrogated and killed the two troops that were stationed there," she informs him as he towers over her, scowling.

"Let me see this," he exclaims.

The woman turns to lead him out of the room. He flicks his cloak, billowing it behind him as he walks. His mind reels with all the terrible things he plans to do to those two cocky rebels. *They have overstepped themselves*, he thinks.

As he enters the room, he slams the door against the wall and glares at everyone who had been startled by his entrance.

"What?" he sneers, "Get back to work." He walks to the front of the room. "Have you identified the two intruders? I want to know their names, where they are, and how quickly we can find them."

"Sir," one man pipes up. "The male is Lieutenant Nova Stargazer, and the female is an unknown hybrid."

"Where is she being held?" Zubenelgenubi asks.

"What do you mean, sir?"

"Where is she being held, she's a hybrid. Where is he? Why is he not with other Constables?" he demands.

The man types for several moments. "They're ghosts."

"What," Zubenelgenubi explodes.

"The rebels must have hacked into our systems and erased all their information," the man explains.

"We need to up our security. I want both of them found and brought in. I want to find out what they know about the rebels," he commands, turning to walk away.

"But, sir. We don't even have any clue as to where they are," the man argues.

"I said to find them, did I not?" he says over his shoulder then exits the room.

I need to find both of them. They could end my reign over Ode, and this girl, this rebel hybrid, she needs to be captured. She is one of the last still free, she could easily lead a rebellion. Ode cannot fall into a planet-wide rebellion. It would end the Council and all my plans.

There is this Constable, however, I must speak to General Vanil about this. I cannot have him running rabid, killing my Constables and rallying the people.

No, Zubenelgenubi stops himself, *let the people rally. Let them think they have a chance. We will make our move in due time and squash this rebellion. That will show them how much power we still have over them,* he thinks.

He continues back to his throne room as he thinks, his mind stuck on the hybrid. *Who can I talk to that will give me insight?* he

68

asks himself.

Then he comes up with the answer, Maaz.

"I must speak with Maaz," he mutters to himself as he continues on his way.

Chapter Thirteen

Ara

I quickly shove things into my bag to prepare for our journey. I wish Messier would tell us how long our missions would take, but he never does for fear of someone having too much information that could be forced out of them. No one, except for Nova, would be able to keep information. Constables could beat it out of most of us.

I finally finish packing my things. I don't really mind going on this mission. However, Nova has expressed clearly how much he does not want to go on this mission. He says he worries about my safety. Truthfully, he should have started thinking about my 'safety' a long time ago. He hasn't seemed to express any interest in protecting me from what is happening in the world around him.

I shoulder my pack, taking a last glance at my room and leave, knowing I may not be back here in a while...or ever.

I weave my way through the rebels who litter the halls of the base. Pushing the door open, I step out into the warm air. Nova waits outside the base, ready to go, but reluctant.

Rebels watch us as we pass by, pausing from their work to nod in our direction. Their solemn looks echo how Nova feels about this mission. He knows the chances of us returning from the Constable base. The chances are probably not all that high.

We finally make it to the pass. The sides loom up above us ominously.

"This doesn't look good," Nova mumbles. Those were the last words he said for a long while. We walk in silence, stumbling over rocks occasionally as we start our hike through a pass in the mountains. I sigh, my feet aching. They couldn't spare an H.P.V. to at least shuttle us to the mountains.

"Ara?" Nova asks as we walk.

"Yes?" I reply, as I shift my bag to the other shoulder.

"Do you want to talk about anything?"

I turn and glare at him, "Seriously? We already had this discussion, Nova."

"You need to talk about what's been happening. You can't continue to bottle everything up until you explode like I used to do." He catches up and walks at my side. "I remember not too long ago, you were chasing me, begging me to talk to you because you didn't want to see me explode. Please, don't be like me, it isn't normal."

"You know what was happening when I was chasing you? My life was still normal, that was before I was thrown into this mess, before I was dragged into your world. I don't like it here. All I want is to go back to the world I was living in, however stupid that sounds. I can't go back there, though. That would end with me dead. You can't expect me to yell and scream when there is no point, there is no hope. Yelling and screaming won't change what is happening, no matter how loud it is. We either finish what we started or we die trying," I exclaim and continue to walk.

"You can't be upset with me forever for not telling you," he says.

"I wasn't talking about that. However, I can be upset with you for however long I want. You should have told me, you knew how I felt about Constables because of what they do to us, to hybrids," I say.

He shrugs, "I was younger. I didn't know what I was doing." He stops, muttering, "I did it for you."

"It wasn't that long ago, Nova. You were hiding things from me, and you still are. Yet you get onto me when I hide things from you. That's not okay. You can't hide things from me if I'm not allowed to hide things from you. There is nothing okay with that," I burst.

Suddenly, I realize he got me to do exactly what he wanted me to do. He provoked me, poked at me and made me burst...made me confide in him.

"See, was that so bad?" he asks. A small smile reaches his lips.

"Nova, stop trying. Stop, because there is no point. I'm not going to try to rekindle a friendship when there is nothing there to light," I sigh and turn away from him to continue to walk.

Slowly, we scale the pass and make it over the mountain. I ignore him most of the time, trying to focus on avoiding rocks and not to trip. I wince as I walk over sharp rocks, my thin shoes offering little protection.

Soon night falls, the air cooling. We begin to search for a lookout position to camp for the night. Suddenly, I see a small building and we go toward it, hoping it is the lookout.

The building appears to be empty so we set up camp there. At least there will be a roof over our heads tonight.

"Do you want to eat?" Nova asks as he sets down his pack and pulls out some of our rations.

I hold my hand out, and he hands me what little food we can have. They couldn't spare much from the rations for this mission. We will have to make do with what we have.

"I'm going to be so happy when we will have enough food that I can have a full meal again," I sigh, as I eat a little.

"That may be for a long time, we don't know how much of the supplies we will be able to get back. If any. Also, we will have to feed more people because of how many we will have to rescue," Nova says.

At least we can hold a conversation without yelling at each other. That seems to be difficult on occasion. There are times when I do think I should forgive him, but I'm not sure. I continue to eat and ignore Nova.

"When we get there, we need to map out the base so we will know where everything and everyone is. It will make it easier to free the prisoners and get the supplies. Without knowing where everything is we could easily get caught and never be able to escape."

"I know Nova, I may be new at this but I have a little common sense," I groan.

"Calm down, Ara. I was telling you to make some conversation so we don't have to sit here in silence all night," Nova says.

I stand. "One of us should stay awake and keep watch in case anything happens. I'll take first watch." I walk over and lean against the door of our small shelter as Nova sighs in frustration.

Oderians don't actually sleep. We rest and lay still. We can zone out into a dream-like state when we rest but it comes nowhere near sleeping like humans do.

After I know Nova is in that state, I slump against the wall. Keeping this act up is going to be hard. It's so difficult for me to act like a person I'm not. Ignoring him, being rude and cold, I don't know how much longer I can do this. Why did I suddenly decide to start acting like this? I have dug myself into a hole I can't get out of because if I stop acting like this he will know something was wrong...He probably already does.

"Ugh," I groan softly. I step outside quietly. I leave the door to the lookout open. The air cools my heated skin.

Sitting down, I look out at the pass. The lookout is positioned perfectly up on a ledge. It has perfect sightline over this entire section. I avert my gaze and look up at the sky, the stars bringing me peace.

My mind starts to wander again as I gaze at the stars. Why does he have to be so frustrating, perceptive, and nice to me right now? I can't figure out if he is truly trying to gain my trust back after what he did. I have to wonder if I should show him that I see what he is doing and try to make him see I am trying to forgive him.

I really am trying to, though. He gives me so many chances to tell him what I am thinking and feeling. He must know this is difficult for me. My entire world has caved in on itself in the last few moons.

I glance back at him through the open doorway, seeing his features calm and serene fills my hearts with joy. Those features that have expressed so much emotion toward me over time but yet those features are scarred with memories of death and murder. His hands that held me when I was upset have killed and tortured. His feet that have been by my side for far too long have walked through many homes prepared to cut down anyone in their path.

I remember a simpler time before I knew he played both sides. We would run around freely, the closest of friends, loving each other's company because there was no reason to do otherwise. We would both stay up long after the sky went black and watch as his glow would grow brighter each second the world around us dimmed.

Sadly, being a hybrid means I have no glow, but before I found out about him, he was my glow. He would light my path for me. He was my hope. He was the reason I got up every day. He was my inspiration and now the Oderian I once knew is gone. He has been replaced by one that is scared with regretted decisions and awful memories of something he can only justify by saying he did it for me. I never asked him to put his life on the line. My father may have, but I would never.

A wave of guilt washes over me. I have heard stories of what the Constables do to new recruits. They beat them and torture them to find out what their pain threshold is. They prod at them with threats of killing the ones they love...

Then it hits me, like a blow to the chest. He actually did do it for me. They probably threatened to hurt me, kill me if he did not join and do as they asked. He knew back then I would not survive long if one came after me. He most likely trained and learned all he did so he could protect me. My hearts ache, how could I have truly been so blind? How does that make me any better than the Constables and the Council who wish to see me dead?

"Oh Nova," I whisper as tears prick at my eyes. I was the reason for the scars on his face and back. I was the reason he became the very cruel, cold hearted monster I hate. In return, I became one too.

Tearing my eyes from the stars, I stand quietly and step back inside the lookout. I close the door without making a sound. Slowly, careful not to pull him from his dream-like state, I walk over to Nova and kneel beside him.

I remember when we would rest next to each other, long after when we should have gone home. His arms would be wrapped around me, his warm glow encasing us both. At some point, I grew to love that feeling. I wanted those nights to last forever. I would look forward to our long nights. I believe I fell in love with him.

Looking at him now, I know the Nova I love is still in there somewhere. I carefully tuck myself under one arm, the same way we used to lay.

I sigh in content and pretend we are back when we had no care in the world and I wasn't a wanted fugitive.

Chapter Fourteen

In the Council Dwellings

"Sir, we have Maaz ready for you whenever you please," the woman states, keeping her eyes to the floor, averted from the back of the new leader of the Council.

Zubenelgenubi nods. "I'll be there in a moment."

He turns from the window in his chambers. He had been enjoying the most recent execution. His eyes gleam with a menacing glow. Watching hybrids die excites him. It is the one thing he has been looking forward to all day.

He pulls himself away from the blood and gore, his cloak sweeping behind him.

The woman waits for him, her eyes still focused on the floor.

"I am ready," he states, weaving his way around a table and chairs.

"Follow me," she breathes, turning and walking out the door.

He trails behind her, in no hurry, knowing this war waits for him to do things as he pleases. He takes his sweet time, not wanting to be short of breath from hurrying when he meets with Maaz. He wants to be as menacing as possible.

He follows the woman down a spiraling staircase, into the depths of the Council Dwellings, through hallways and doors even he had never seen before. It gets darker, and suddenly his glow kicks on. The narrow hallway is bathed in a soft blue light.

The woman stops in front of a large door, her hands folded in front of her.

"We are here. He is inside. Two Constables are there to

control things in case he gets out of hand," she says.

Zubenelgenubi nods, not bothering to thank the woman. He has better things to do.

He opens the door, squinting, and steps into the bright room. His eyes adjust quickly.

"Sir," the two Constables greet him.

He nods in their general direction, his eyes set on the older Oderian who sits at the table in front of him. Wrinkles have started to adorn his face, bags showing plainly underneath his eyes, moons of restless nights catching up to him.

"Former Councilman Maaz, what a pleasure to meet with you," Zubenelgenubi sneers, as he sits down at the table.

"Trust me, if I had a choice, I would never even have to look at you," Maaz replies with little interest.

A mischievous smile creeps across Zubenelgenubi's face. "You are going to want to look at me. You knew much about hybrids during your time on the Council."

"I knew much about many things." Maaz eyes Zubenelgenubi. "What do you want, you tyrant? You wouldn't come all the way down here if you didn't have a reason." The skin around his eyes wrinkles as he insults the Oderian.

"I have a small problem with a hybrid. She seems to be working with Nova Stargazer and the rebels. What do you know?" Zubenelgenubi questions.

Maaz's eyes go wide, his emotions betraying him. "I-I don't know anything about that."

"You are lying," Zubenelgenubi sneers, slamming his fist down on the table. Maaz knows something, he can tell. "Tell me."

"I don't have to tell you anything," Maaz says through gritted teeth.

"You see, but you do. Your daughter is a hybrid, correct? As far as I know she hasn't been executed...yet." Zubenelgenubi leans back in his chair, knowing this will incentivize the Oderian to speak.

Maaz is silent, glaring at Zubenelgenubi, his face contorted in disgust.

Zubenelgenubi shrugs, turning to the Constable nearest to him, "Go find me his daughter."

The Constable nods and leaves the small room in a rush, knowing what is on the line if his task is not completed in a timely manner.

"Now, are you going to tell me what you know or will I have to schedule a special execution for your daughter? I already killed your wife years ago. We can make it a family tradition." Zubenelgenubi grins, folding his hands on the table.

Seconds later the Constable steps back into the room, deathly pale.

"Sir," he starts, "We don't have her in custody."

"What do you mean we don't have her in custody?" Zubenelgenubi's smile is forced now. *How could she not be in the custody of the Council?*

"She didn't show up in the database, sir," the Constable says.

Zubenelgenubi's hands ball up into fists, without warning he flies into a fit of rage. He snatches the staff from the other Constable, breaks the globe on the floor and runs the Constable through with it. Zubenelgenubi's lip twitches as he twists the staff inside the Constable. The Constable's face contorts in pain, his eyes rolling up into his head and he slowly slides down the wall, leaving blood smeared all the way down.

Maaz sits calmly as he watches the scene unfold in front of him. This doesn't surprise him. A tyrant would kill the messenger of bad news.

"Now," growls Zubenelgenubi, as he turns back around, the crazed gleam still lingering in his eyes. One eyelid twitches, the blood splatter slowly dripping down his cheeks like bloody tears. "What do you know?" He slams his hands down on the table again, this time covered in blood, leaving smudged handprints on the once pristine table.

"I won't tell you anything. You have nothing." Maaz leans forward into Zubenelgenubi's face. "In time you will understand, I am nothing but a pawn in a much larger game. Open your eyes and see the world for what it really is now. You need to come to terms with the interbreeding of Oderians and Humans. Hybrids are unavoidable."

"Stop arguing for them, they are mutts, scum, mistakes of two separate species. They must be eliminated," Zubenelgenubi exclaims.

"They aren't. They are the gentlest beings I have ever met," Maaz sighs.

His eyes narrow, slowly putting the pieces together. "You aren't worried about your daughter, are you? In fact, you know exactly where she is."

Maaz shrugs, refusing to answer any more questions posed by the tyrannical leader.

"Your daughter is the hybrid I'm after. She went and joined the rebellion." A pleased smirk crawls across Zubenelgenubi's face. "What a Daddy's girl, working for the good of her kind. Do you know who she is with?"

"Nova Stargazer and I wouldn't have it any other way," Maaz whispers harshly.

"Oh yes, the infamous Nova Stargazer. The stone-cold killer. He has no feelings. He doesn't care about what happens to your daughter one bit. You know that, right?" Zubenelgenubi stands, his bloody hands still in place on the table. "In fact, he probably has more blood on his hands than I do on mine, and I've killed a lot of people."

"Nova Stargazer would never betray me or Ara." Maaz leans forward again, "You know nothing of the real Nova."

Zubenelgenubi laughs, "Oh I know plenty. His reputation precedes him. Let me see...He was up for General more than once, the youngest ever, I do believe. In fact, he was trained by General Vanil himself. Now, we all know General Vanil is a hardened killer and hand picks students who remind him of himself."

Maaz snickers, "You have no idea of whom you have made an enemy. If you dare to hurt a single hair on Ara's head, Nova will hunt you down and kill you more brutally than you killed that Constable over there." He motions to the body of the Constable slumped against the wall. "There will be no escaping the hell he will unleash upon you."

"I know what hell looks like former Councilman, you nor Nova will scare me enough to give up on what I want Ode to become," Zubenelgenubi huffs, turning his back to Maaz. "Before long your daughter and Nova Stargazer will be in my custody. There will be nothing you can do about it. I will enjoy watching her hang."

Maaz jumps to his feet, launching himself after Zubenelgenubi, and the remaining Constable latches onto him, holding him back. "If you touch her I swear…" Maaz starts.

"You'll what? Kill me? Good luck with that," Zubenelgenubi interjects, shrugging.

"You can't do this. It isn't right. Think for a moment," Maaz shouts, struggling against the Constable.

Zubenelgenubi ignores him, speaking over his shoulder to the Constable, "Take him to base four-fifty-two. Make sure when we catch the hybrid and Stargazer they are taken to the same base," he pauses, smiling. "What a bloody reunion that will be." He then turns back to the door.

"Stop this, please. Don't hurt her, please," Maaz begs as Zubenelgenubi walks out the door.

The door slams shut, and Zubenelgenubi can still hear Maaz's pleas for mercy on his daughter. His boots echo with each step down the hall, every step putting him closer to catching Stargazer and the hybrid, putting him closer to everything he has ever wanted.

Chapter Fifteen

Ara

Slowly I open my eyes and slip out from under Nova's arm before he leaves his dream state. He can't know I what did last night, besides I couldn't face him like that. Not yet anyway. Too much has happened to pretend everything's back to normal. I sit for a moment, thinking, if all of this had never happened, what would I be doing right now?

I take a deep breath. I would be going for a run with Nova. I would go home, like any other day, repetitive and endlessly dull. It's what I would have done every day for the past several moons instead of train, instead of go on missions, instead of being persecuted.

I stand and stretch for a moment. My muscles ache from all the work yesterday; the ache gets stronger every time I move. Finally, I groan in pain as I lean down and shake Nova, pulling him out of his dream state.

He sighs and opens his silver eyes. "You were in your dream state all night," I say as I straighten up wincing and slowly hobbling over to my pack.

"Why didn't you wake me to take over on watch?" he says gruffly, his voice hoarse from little use.

"You looked like you needed rest," I say, with my back turned towards him as I dig through my pack hoping he didn't know what I did.

"So, you stayed up the entire night on watch?" he asks. "Aren't you exhausted?"

"No, I was able to sleep a little," I say, as I stand and shoulder my pack, trying to hold in my groans of pain.

He sighs, "Alright." He picks up his bag and quickly packs up all his belongings. "We need to get going or else we will get behind which would completely throw off the entire plan."

"Thus, the reason why I got you up." I roll my eyes and step out of our small shelter.

I take a deep breath of the damp, cool air. At least today will be cool. I glance up at the sky and see a large cloud looming over the pass. Looks like we get to hike in the rain.

Nova steps out and sees the cloud. "Wonderful," he groans.

"A little water never hurt anyone." I shrug and begin to walk, kicking up the dry dust.

Every step I take, the ache seems to intensify. Eventually, it gets to be worse than right after I started running with Nova. My steps get smaller and harder to take as we walk. Soon, Nova is in the lead, being able to walk faster and take bigger steps.

He walks for a while until he turns back to me. "Why are you walking so slowly? We can't stick around to see the sights, we have to move quickly."

I force a smile, "I am currently walking as fast as I can."

"Why?" He stops walking, after a few moments I catch up to him.

"I am unbelievably sore," I answer as lower myself down onto a rock, resting.

"Why exactly are you sore?" Nova asks me, kneeling down in front of me.

I shrug, "I don't have the slightest idea." I lift my leg up, trying to carefully stretch the muscle. "Ow." I hiss. "That hurts...A lot."

"Rest for a bit. We will continue here in a little while," Nova sighs.

We sit in silence. All I hear is the soft rustle of an occasional breeze.

"So, did anything interesting happen while you were on watch?" he asks, breaking the silence.

"Not really," I say. "I sat outside for a while, looked at the stars. Nothing too exciting."

He nods, "So you did nothing strenuous?"

"No." I shake my head. It's true, physically I sat there, all the work I was doing was in my head.

"I don't know why you are sore then. Maybe it's from all the walking yesterday." Nova glances away for a moment. "Alright, you have had your rest, let's get you on your feet and moving."

He offers his hand to help me up. I take it and he pulls me to my feet. My muscles protest with the painful ache once again.

"Let's go," I huff through tight lips.

If I complain too much then I know Nova will make me rest again. If we take too long resting, we mess up the timeline. So, I walk and deal with the pain. After a while it fades out, then comes back full force and repeats in a never-ending cycle of pain.

My eyes set themselves on the massive cloud that takes over the horizon. Soon, I can see nothing beyond it. As we approach the cloud, the sounds around us seem to fade away, and all I can hear as we walk is the sound of our footsteps. The crunching of the dirt beneath our boots seems to echo and bounce off the walls of the pass.

The cloud continues to loom over us, growing ever larger.

"This may be a bad storm," Nova says as we continue to walk.

"I would say we should hunker down in a shelter. However, there isn't one near us, and that would also throw off the entire timeline of the plan," I say, knowing that would never happen.

"We should keep going. I think we can push ourselves through it," Nova responds, not missing a step as he stares at the sky.

I stiffen up as there is a flash across the cloud and a loud crack.

"Wow," Nova gasps.

We keep walking even as it begins to rain. Soon we stand in the middle of the storm.

"This is beautiful," I yell over the sound of the thunder. "And exceedingly frightening all at the same time."

The storm seems to swirl above us. The lightning seems to flash constantly. The deep green clouds breathe, churning, growing larger then shrinking.

Suddenly the wind picks up. A stray strand of my hair whips in it. A gust pushes the hood of my cloak up and over my head, covering my eyes. I tear it off. It is getting increasingly hard to see.

"Look. Ara, we need to go. Now," Nova yells over the sound of thunder, but I can barely hear him because his voice is stolen by the wind.

I turn to see what Nova meant. My eyes land on a huge dust cloud coming toward us. It must have been blown up by the wind. The dust starts to swirl like the clouds.

"Oh, that's not good," I mutter.

Nova snatches up my hand and pulls me along behind him, running. There is no way we could ever outrun that thing. It seems to move faster even as we run away. No one, no matter how fast they are could ever outrun that monster of a dust storm.

"Nova," I yell. "We need to find shelter. We can't outrun that."

"I know. That's why we're running," he yells back.

"To where?" I screech, all my hair now whipping around my face.

"I don't know." He slides to a halt, looking along the edge of the pass for something, anything.

I scan the walls of the pass. A large crack catches my eye. I squint, trying to make out what it is through all the dust the wind is kicking up. For a moment I can't tell, then I realize that it is a cave.

"There," I scream over the wind that seems to be growing louder with every passing moment.

Nova turns, grabbing my hand again and we fight against the wind, trying to get to the cave. We make it there as the wind picks up even more. Nova takes off his cloak and stretches it out across the opening, stuffing the corners in the cracks to hold it.

"That should keep some of the dust out," he says over the wind.

I sit down against the wall and brush the sand and dust out of my hair. I carefully get it out my eyes. Nova does the same.

I continue to brush the dust away, realizing the storm took my attention away from my sore body. Nova quickly finishes removing the sand and dirt. He hops to his feet and starts pacing the small cave from end to end.

"Why are you pacing?" I ask as I finish.

"This is going to completely throw off the entire time line," he sighs, clearly frustrated.

"So? Don't all plans go a little wayward? I mean, you can't expect everything to go perfectly to plan. There is no point in stressing about it. Everything will be fine as long as we do stick to the plan as much as possible and don't get completely thrown off track. Come on," I sigh. "When you were a Constable didn't some plans get so screwed up you had to abandon them and come up with a whole new one with its own whole new set of problems?"

Nova stares at me. "When did you become so wise?"

I shrug and stare at the wall of the dim cave. I stretch out my legs, my toes touching the other wall of the cave. It may offer some protection, but it's cramped.

The wind continues to blow outside for quite some time. After it stops we hear the rain pound and the thunder continue to rumble ominously, as if daring us to step outside into the storm again.

I start to stand but Nova places his hand on my shoulder stopping me.

"There is no point in going out there. Another dust storm could form at any time and we may not be fortunate enough to find another place to shelter in," he warns.

I slide back down the wall. Nova lowers himself down next to me.

For a while he stares at me. I sit there ignoring him until I can't take it anymore, and I close my eyes, resting. Even with my eyes shut tightly, I can still feel his eyes on me.

Without opening them I turn my head and ask, "Why are you looking at me so intently? Do I still have sand in my hair or something? Did I say something I shouldn't have?"

"No, I..." he falters. I open my eyes, his silver ones meeting mine, then he looks away.

"Why?" I ask again.

"Why did you lay with me last night?" he asks without missing a beat.

My eyes go wide, how did he know?

"How- how?" I stutter, nervous about where this will be going. I look away from him, embarrassed.

"As a Constable, I-I learned how to make myself look like I am in a dream state. It proves to be useful at times. You were worrying me last night. I could tell you were having problems with something. To be honest, I thought you were going to stay outside looking at the stars all night," he explains.

"I was thinking about how we used to lay like that and stay up late into the night, talking and laughing," I pause, the memories flying past my eyes again, "I missed that. I wanted a reminder of a time when we weren't running, when we weren't doing crazy missions and fighting a war that doesn't need to happen," I admit.

What else am I supposed to do? He would know that I was lying if I didn't tell him, and if I lied it wouldn't make me any better than him.

He looks at me for a moment, realizing I do want to forgive him, I don't hate him like he originally thought. Things are...complicated. Everything is complicated.

"I'm sorry Ara, I truly am. I wish I could stop this war. The one way to do that is if we help the rebels. We have to make sure both the Council and Zubenelgenubi are punished for their horrid crimes a thousand times over. I will do all of that for you," he whispers, his hand cupping one side of my face.

His silver eyes seem to say the thousands of words he can't get out. Everything he has been longing to tell these last few moons is all conveyed by the tiny glint in his bright silver eyes.

For one gleaming moment I don't want to leave this cave, I want to stay here, with Nova by my side to keep me company, to tell all my crazy ideas and stories to. Everyone needs someone like that. Maybe, someday soon I can do that, sit with Nova by my side and the world at peace. I could spend the rest of my existence in a world where I could do that.

I reach up and push his hand away. I will never get to do that if we don't finish this mission and every one after.

I glance up at him, and he almost looks hurt by my denial of his touch. Though I long to comfort him, now is not the time. We have to think about the mission. If we get distracted, like he has told me a thousand times, one of us will get hurt.

"How much further do we have to go?" I ask as I look away, unable to look at his pained eyes any longer.

"We have to make it through the pass. Then we will meet up with the undercover operatives from the Constable base. From there, we will go with them," Nova pauses, thinking. "It should take us about another day or so to make it through the pass," he answers, his voice slowly becoming stronger as he talks, suppressing his pain.

This makes my heart ache again. There was a time when I would do anything to stop that ache. No matter what. There was a time when I stayed up and watched him rest with that beautiful peaceful look on his face. I would imagine his lips pressed against my own, knowing that scenario would never happen outside my own mind. So, I do what he does now, I suppress the pain along with the feeling, no matter how strong it is.

I swallow hard, pulling myself out of those memories. "That's good. I want to get this mission over and done with as soon as possible so we can win this pitiful war."

Nova gives me an amused look. "Why is it pitiful? I thought you said that it was horrid?"

"Either way it is a pointless war, the Council and Zubenelgenubi want to rile up the people so they can blame the hybrid genocide on someone else and then sweep in and save the day. Fixing their image and reputation, making everyone love them again. They are trying to give more proof as to why we need them. Why Ode can't function on its own, without them. It truly is pitiful." I glare at Nova.

He smiles, amused by my comments and shakes his head, "Such strong opinions you're forming."

"Is there a problem with that?" I ask.

"No," he answers quickly.

I huff and roll my eyes, "I know what you're thinking Stargazer, so don't think I'm not onto you."

He gasps in mock hurt. "How could you ever accuse me of such a thing?"

"Don't say I didn't warn you," I shrug.

Suddenly there is a huge gust of wind, making me flinch. Sand flutters into the cave through a small gap between Nova's cloak and the wall of the cave. "I'm glad we didn't go back out there."

Nova nods, "Yes, besides I think we both need a little extra rest."

I nod in agreement and lean my head against the wall of the cave. "How could these mountains not have been explored by the Council or anyone in fact? Are Oderians so closed minded, determined to live in their tiny sheltered society they do not want to discover and learn about the real world around them?"

"The Council believes exploration is not needed until we must expand our cities." Nova shrugs.

"Screw the Council. I want to see Ode. I want to learn about the wonders of my world. My mother said before they had to leave Earth they explored the entire planet. There were oceans and lands covered in ice and sand. There were ruins of ancient civilizations that built great temples to honor gods. There were forests and cities made of stone. Paths connected every place. Oh, she told me about how they had a piece of technology used to talk to people, you could press a button and see the person you were talking too. Even if they were on the other side of the planet," I exclaim.

Nova laughs. "You sound as if you have been there yourself."

"If that were possible, I certainly would. Ode is still here though, and we should explore it to the fullest extent. We should learn about the world we live in, so when our planet dies we can travel and tell stories of our world to other people," I sigh.

"Maybe we've been cooped up in here for too long," Nova says, jokingly.

I hit his arm and scowl at him. I think this is the best terms we have been on in a while. Maybe things are starting to look a little better. "You are terrible."

"Only when you are here with me," he grins.

"I think the storm is starting to die down out there," I say as I stand and move the pinned-up cloak slightly to peek outside. The rain seems to be coming down softly now, and the clouds aren't nearly as dark as they were earlier.

"I think we should stay here for the night," Nova says softly as he peeks outside from beside me.

"Are you sure? It will set us back by a day if not more." I turn towards him.

"Yes, there's no point. We wouldn't make very much progress. There's not enough daylight left to even get to the next shelter. The operatives will have to wait another day," he shrugs.

"Alright, if you say so, but good luck resting without using your cloak as a pillow because I'm not letting you take that thing down in case another storm blows up some dust," I say as I walk back into the cave and lean against the wall.

"I guess I will have to live with it," he sighs as he turns toward me, his glow sending shadows creeping across the wall and ceiling.

I slide down the wall. "I guess I better get comfortable. We're going to be here a while. You should too."

Nova nods and sits back down next to me.

"Do you remember the time we decided the best place to lay and look at the stars was on your roof?" Nova asks softly, shifting around in an effort to get into a somewhat comfortable spot.

"I remember. We laid there all night, then when we were about to climb down you almost fell off the roof. I have to admit, though, it was pretty funny," I grin.

"I made sure never to lay that close to the edge ever again." He nods.

"It couldn't have been that bad." I laugh.

"Well, you weren't the one who almost fell to their death. I could never forget the feeling of dangling by my fingertips, it was so much fun," he huffs, his sarcastic tone echoing through the cave.

I roll my eyes. "That's true, but I wouldn't have let you fall to your death. Don't be dramatic."

"That's also true." Nova leans his head against the wall of the cave.

Being cooped up in here has forced me to get back on to better terms with Nova. Maybe that storm was meant to happen so we would be stuck in here together. I don't think Nova and I have had an easy conversation since I found out that he had been a Constable.

"Nova, can I ask you something?" I ask, breaking the short moment of silence.

"Shoot," he says.

"How did you hide the fact that you were a Constable from me? That can't have been easy." I glance up at him to see his reaction. He had to have known I would ask him this question at some point.

He sighs and looks away. "I got myself into a lot of trouble at times because I would sneak off to meet up with you at the regular times so it wouldn't seem like anything was wrong. I remember being late a few times. I had to lie to you about where I was or what I was doing. It was difficult. There were a few instances where I was on probation. I wasn't allowed to leave the bunks but I would still somehow find a way to sneak off."

"Why, though? Why did you join?" I ask.

"I joined because I thought I was protecting you. I thought I was protecting you from a greater evil, but I wasn't. All I ended up doing was bring out the evil in myself. I eventually realized one day you would find out about that evil. I was scared at times because I was still a Constable when you started to hate them," he says, still not looking at me.

"Of course I started to hate them. They murdered three hybrid children," I exclaim.

He nods. "I know. I had no part in that. After a while I started moving up. I was a Commander at one point, and I almost became General. I could have led the entire Constable force, but I started disappearing more often to make sure you were okay because the murdering of hybrids was getting worse. I was demoted several times. Not that I cared, I wanted to make sure you were alright. Yes, I did hurt many people and I regret it. There is not a day that goes by when I do not think about the people I hurt, the children who no longer have parents because I was a cruel monster. I do regret it. "

I stay silent for a moment. He did it for me.

"You became the very monster I hate, because of me." A lump rises in my throat, a wave of guilt washes over me. I had suspicions but needed to know for sure.

"I didn't have a choice. What was I going to do? Watch you bleed to death because a Constable stabbed you? I wanted to keep you safe and keep you alive because no one as innocent as you deserved to die like that," he argues.

"You could have run. You could have disappeared. I would have gotten over it," I argue back.

"No. I couldn't have. I, me, I could not have lived with myself if I had left you to fend for yourself." He points to himself, then turns his finger on me, poking my arm. "Besides, you know damn well it would have killed you to have me go missing," he hisses.

"It would have been better that finding out you were a monster," I snap, immediately regretting the words the moment they came out of my mouth.

"Would a monster be sitting here next to you? If I was truly as much of a monster as other Constables, you would be dead right now. I would have strangled you or bashed your head in with a rock. I could have knocked you out and left you here to die. I could have left you in that sandstorm to suffocate," he snarls, standing up.

He towers over me as I still sit on the ground. I shrink back slightly, but still continue to push, knowing I shouldn't make him any more upset. "Then why don't you? Hmm? Why don't you revert back to your old ways? Kill me and Pandra, go back to your commanders. You would be considered a hero. You killed the last hybrids. The war is over. Have a great rest of your life 'Mr. I'm a Hero because I killed the last two hybrids'."

He seems to physically restrain himself. I think he knows I am testing him to see how far I can go before he snaps back into the monstrous ways of a Constable.

"You," he points a finger at me, his lips twitching, "Need to stop. You are going to get yourself killed if you mess with every Constable like that. Some would have already killed you."

I shrug. "I wanted to know how far I could push you. Most Constables aren't very level headed."

"I know, but I'm not like most Constables." He turns away and leans against the opposite wall. "You need to stop pushing so hard Ara because one day you are going to end up getting on the wrong side of me. I'm going to blow up and end up hurting you."

I roll my eyes. "Do you really think that's going to stop me? Wouldn't you have done it before now? Why would you hurt me now?"

"I'm warning you," he sighs.

"I'm sure you are, but I don't need a warning. I know what your temper is like nowadays. You used to be very level headed but ever since you became a Constable your temper has been uncontrollable. I know when not to push you, Nova. I know you better than you think," I shrug.

"No, no you don't," he exclaims. "I was a different person as a Constable. I was the worst version of myself. I was cruel. I had no feelings. I killed for the rush. I looked down on people as if they were below me. That's the kind of person that is hidden away inside me. That's the Nova I never want to see again, so if you wouldn't mind, please stop trying to pull him out of me because, believe it or not, you don't want to meet him." He tears his cloak off the entrance of the cave and storms right out.

"Alright then," I mutter to myself, as I stand and slowly follow him outside. I watch as he picks up rocks and hurls them at the walls of the pass. He kicks at the wall and bangs his fists against it trying to take out all his anger he has bottled up. That was what I was trying to release. Maybe if he had a chance to let everything out, he would calm down some. He pulls at his hair and runs his hand across his face several times before he falls to his knees and holds his face in his hands. The rain soaks his clothes and streams from his hair.

I walk over to him and listen as he mutters to himself, "I'm sorry, I'm sorry. I made a mistake. I'm so sorry."

I carefully kneel down next to him and wrap an arm around his figure. "I know. It's okay. You don't have to apologize anymore. I forgive you." He seems to tense up for a moment but then relaxes as I pull him against me. It's a new thing to see him reveal a more helpless side of himself to anyone. He always tried to hide and act tough so he wouldn't upset me, but I can tell he needed to do something like this for years. He needed to let it all go. Too many times has he been there for me but I never had the chance to return the favor because he could never forget his pride enough to show a gentler side to his personality.

"You don't hate me?" he whispers, childishly.

"No, Nova. I don't hate you. I wouldn't be right here if I did." I give him a forgiving smile. He wraps his arms around my waist in a protective manner. We sit there for a while, arms around each other, not sure if we were fighting, if we made up, or if the events that occurred even truly happened. For a while, I felt like things were back to the way they should be. I believe as we sat there we both wanted to take back most of the things that were said. We didn't mean any of them, but we both know we got carried away in the moment.

"We should go back to the cave," Nova says as it starts to get dark. "There is no telling what is out here that could kill us."

I nod and stand. I would rather not be eaten alive by some crazy animal that comes out at night. I shiver, the dampness of the rain starting to set in. Nova stands then pulls me up to my feet and we head back to our little cave.

"Nova, what if we were to disappear? I'm sure that we could live off the land. We could get away from the rebels, the Council, Zubenelgenubi, and the war. We could live our own lives deep in the mountains and not ever have to worry about being found. Besides, if I was to disappear, Pandra would be the last hybrid. Do you think the war would end if there was one left? Or would we take her with us?" I think out loud as we walk.

"We would have to leave Pandra behind, and we would always be running Ara. They wouldn't stop searching until they knew you were dead." Nova rolls his eyes as if it were obvious.

"Then why don't we fake my death? We could do it at the base and escape back to the rebels. We could have one of the operatives kill me during our get away and no one would be the wiser," I say the second it popped into my head.

"That's not a bad idea. I could easily carry you out. The question is, how we would fake the silver from your eyes because that would be the selling point that you were truly dead." Nova nods as we get back to the cave.

We walk in and I say, "We could kill a Constable then use his silver. The operative could say he caught me trying to sneak away and killed me then caught the silver in a vile. No one would be able to tell that the silver wasn't mine because my body would be gone."

Nova leans against the side of the cave, thinking. "It might work. That would pull you out of their minds, and it would stop their search for you and me. They would be hunting for me, and me alone, which would make it much more difficult for them because I would be a lot harder to catch. They know it will be almost impossible to find me, so they would probably give up."

"So, do you think it would be worth trying?" I ask as I sit down again.

"It would be worth a try. However, you wouldn't be able to go on any other missions because that would ruin the plan, but you would be able to stay at the base until the war is over. You would be much safer in the base than out on missions. Plus, if our current mission is successful then it may be over much sooner than we thought it would be," Nova explains.

"That's fine. I hate going on these stupid missions anyway. I would like to actually make it through the war and go home. I'm afraid on one of these missions I'm going to end up dead for real and that would be it," I say softly.

"That's not going to happen because we are going to fake your death," Nova says.

"Yes," I laugh. "We will fake it, not actually cause it. There's going to have to be some serious acting on your part."

"Yes, but I think I will be able to handle it." He sits down too. "I think we should rest. We will have a long way to go tomorrow, and we don't want to worry about being exhausted the entire time we are walking."

I curl up against the wall of the cave, using my pack as a pillow. I quickly eat a little bit of our dried food then lay down.

"Thank you, Ara," Nova whispers after a while. He must have thought that I had gone into a dream state. I can hear him come closer and sit down next to me. "All I want to do is protect you, and I would give anything to do that, no matter what the cost. Even if it is my own life."

I flinch when I feel his hand brush lightly against my hair. He pulls back and stays silent for a moment, waiting to make sure he didn't pull me from the dream state. He brushes a hand against my hair again then gets up to take watch.

Chapter Sixteen

In the Council Dwellings

Zubenelgenubi leans back into his throne, sighing. Who knew planning genocide and waiting for it to play out could be so incredibly dull.

After his enlightening conversation with Maaz, he had been pondering what to do with the former Councilman, seeing as how he is useless now that Zubenelgenubi got everything he wanted out of the Oderian. Everything he came up with so far was either entirely too bloody, even though blood is one of Zubenelgenubi's favorite things, not bloody enough, or not painful enough.

Zubenelgenubi sighs, rubbing his temples. He's giving himself a headache overthinking this whole ordeal.

What do I do with Maaz? He asks himself again.

His entire plan rests on getting the hybrid girl and Stargazer. All he wants is for a lot of blood to be shed, but not the hybrid's, she is going to be executed in front of the entire planet. It couldn't be Stargazer's either, no, he needed to be punished by General Vanil for his treason against the Constables and the Council. So, the truly expendable one is Maaz. It will be his blood spilled, but how to do it?

The door to the throne room creaks open.

"What do you want?" Zubenelgenubi snaps, not thrilled about being interrupted from his thoughts.

"General Vanil wants to speak with you," the Councilwoman tells him.

Zubenelgenubi groans. "Exactly what I need." He stands, straightening his Tan Dew, then sits back down. "Alright, let him in."

General Vanil steps into the room in silence. He piercing eyes fall on Zubenelgenubi. "Sir," he nods in the Oderian's direction.

"What do you want, General Vanil?" Zubenelgenubi sits back on his throne.

"I heard you were looking into Nova Stargazer," the General says.

"I am," Zubenelgenubi nods. "What do you know?"

"Everything," the General answers. "What do you want to know?"

"I want to know everything. What are his weaknesses? Who does he care about? How much does he know?" Zubenelgenubi leans forward in his throne, a twisted smile forming on his face. "How much do you know about the hybrid he has been spotted with?"

The General nods, "I will start from the beginning then."

"Please do." Zubenelgenubi shifts slightly, getting comfortable in his chair.

"Stargazer joined the ranks quite a few moons ago. He knew nothing and all he wanted to do was train. He learned everything from one trainer, beat them in battle, then moved on to the next one. Eventually, he caught my eye," General Vanil explains.

"Ah, so you knew him personally," Zubenelgenubi prods.

"In a way, he was my student for a long time." General Vanil turns from his leader for a moment. "He was young. I don't think he quite knew what he was getting himself into at the time, but I know he wanted it. He wanted it bad, and he was going to do anything to get there."

"He is dedicated then," Zubenelgenubi nods.

"He is very dedicated. For the longest time, he would come to training, learn what he needed to then leave, run off to some place." The General sighs.

"Was he going to meet someone?" the leader of the Council asks, intrigued.

"I followed him once. He met up with a young hybrid. In fact, the hybrid daughter of former Councilman Maaz. They would meet and climb up onto the roof of her house. They would stay up there all night. He pointed out stars to her. When morning came, they would say their goodbyes, and he would come to training. I don't know when he ever actually rested because I heard he would do that almost every day. I have no idea how he could make it through training so exhausted every single day for moons." The General turns back around, deep in thought.

"I have heard he climbed the ladder of ranks rather quickly," Zubenelgenubi states.

General Vanil nods, "He was an excellent Constable. He never lost a fight, to my knowledge. Officers would battle him for fun, knowing their positions were on the line when they did so. He would defeat them, and they would have to give up their position to him. Stargazer would fight them one after another. Everyone wanted to battle him because they wanted to be the person to defeat him."

"Was he well liked? Was he strict in those positions of power?" Zubenelgenubi asks, now deep in thought too.

"He had certain ways of doing things. He was very meticulous about how he ran things. He always made sure he was able to get back in time to meet with his hybrid," the General answers.

"Now, did the hybrid know what he was doing?"

General Vanil shakes his head, "She did not. He never told her. I can assume why, I know she voiced rather strong opinions about how she felt about Constables."

"Interesting," Zubenelgenubi breathes.

"He stayed in a high position of command for several moons. Many wanted him to battle me for General, but he wouldn't. Eventually, he started showing up less and less. He was demoted several times because he wouldn't show up for duty. I believe it was because he was worried about his hybrid friends, seeing as how that was as you, sir, were starting to take power," the General explains.

"So, he was worried about her safety. Are they together?" Zubenelgenubi asks as confusion takes over the Oderian's face.

The General shrugs now, "I do not believe so. I think he is in love with her, whether he has admitted it to himself or not, and he is dedicated to her."

"That," Zubenelgenubi stands, "Is a potential weakness in an Oderian that has practically none."

"It is," the General nods. "He quit showing up for duty one day, and I haven't been able to catch him since then. He moves around with the hybrid a lot, and he knows all the insides and outs of our operation. He would know exactly when there are patrols and how to avoid them."

"He did a very good job of that. Did you not send Constables after him to bring him back?" Zubenelgenubi asks.

"He managed to avoid them all. He knew exactly what we were going to do before we even did it. He knew too much and was too careful to be caught. He is smart," the General sighs.

"Now he has been smart enough to join the rebels with that hybrid of his. The former Constable you couldn't catch is now causing me major problems. I need to get rid of him and that hybrid somehow." Zubenelgenubi slumps back down into his throne.

"Do you have some way to send a message?" the General asks. "The hybrid probably isn't nearly as strong mentally as Stargazer is. Hurt someone, threaten to do something. Scare her. Stargazer will be sure to try and comfort her in any way possible."

Zubenelgenubi's face lights up, "I have her father."

"Former Councilman Maaz?" General Vanil asks, planting his feet in shock.

"Yes, I will break her and in breaking her, I will break Stargazer." Zubenelgenubi grins menacingly. "Her father will die before her eyes. She already watched her mother die, let me add her father and every single other person she cares about. Except for Stargazer, she will watch him turn back into the Constable he used to be. Restored to his former glory. Oh, she will hate that."

The General nods, mulling over his leader's plan in his head. "That would certainly do it."

"I can imagine it. Her father standing there, then he gets run through by a Constable, hell maybe by Stargazer. I can see her face as he bleeds out on the floor. His silver will intermingle with his own blood. His silver won't be caught. Dishonoring him will drive her mad. She will turn on Stargazer and he will have no choice but to come crawling back to the

Council, back to me, back to you General Vanil." Zubenelgenubi stands, walking down the steps from his throne.

He sets his hands on the shoulders of General Vanil, "This is how we will end them both. This is how we will end the rebels."

Chapter Seventeen

Ara

"Ara, you need to get up. We really need to get going. The operatives are waiting for us, and we don't want to make them wait too long. They could contact the rebels thinking we died on the way there," Nova says.

I slowly sit up, groaning as I do, my body more sore than yesterday from being cooped up in the small space of the cave. I take a deep breath and stretch.

Nova leans against the side of the cave, smirking. "Problem?"

"No." I glared up at him. I stand and grab my pack, eating a little once again. I know I have to keep my strength up. "Have you eaten anything, Nova?" I ask.

He shakes his head and walks out of the cave. I quickly follow him. "You really should eat. You will need your energy." I fall into step next to him. "Here, you can have the rest." I offer him what was left of the nutrition bar I had been eating.

"We will not have enough supplies to last us if we both continue eating like we have been and if we continue to run into trouble," he says, his pack already on his shoulder.

"Take it, Nova," I force it into his hand.

He sighs and eats what was left of it. "You really shouldn't be this selfless in this type of situation. You should be focused on your own survival."

I roll my eyes, "Says the one who hasn't eaten anything and should be worrying about his own survival if he was taking his own advice."

He glares at me as he continues to walk. "I…" He stops himself, realizing he had been backed into a corner.

"Gotcha," I laugh as I continue walking.

He rolls his eyes and shakes his head. "Your use of English slang is killing me. You have been around Pandra too much, and she has been around certain humans too much."

We walk for hours on end, my feet starting to hurt from our days of moving. I am going to be glad when I can sit down and not be worried about how I am going to live through the next mission. After a while, we sight an H.P.V. and several Oderians at the end of the pass.

We make our way up to them quickly, knowing that time is running short.

"We are glad you made it through the pass alive, very few can do that, especially because of the storm that blew up yesterday," one says as he shakes Nova's hand.

"We were lucky enough to sight a cave near us and took shelter to wait it out. We wouldn't have made it otherwise," Nova explains.

"We better get going. We will raise more suspicion the longer we are out here. The plan is to take you in under the pretense that you had been snooping and we spotted you while on patrol. We will take you to the cells where the other prisoners are being held, which is on the farthest side of the building. The supplies are on the other side. When you break out you will have to fight your way to the other side, however, many of the prisoners are soldiers for the rebellion, so you will not be alone in your efforts. There will be two H.P.V.s near the supplies. You can load one with the freed prisoners and the other with the rations. Those will be able to get you out of the base faster," he explains quickly.

He then leads us onto the H.P.V., knocking on the door to signal the pilot to take off. Seconds later we are in the air, moving swiftly over the flat land. Within moments we sight the base off in the distance.

"We will have to make you appear as prisoners so I will have to secure you both." He pulls out two short metal rods.

"Be careful with these on Ara. If you struggle to much they

will shock you. Put your hands behind you and relax," Nova instructs as he turns around, placing his hands behind him.

As the Oderian holds the rod in the space between his hands, a red ring forms around his wrists and connects to the rod.

"Wow..." I gasp as I watch.

"They were testing these when I was still a Constable. They are nearly impossible to escape from," Nova says as the Oderian puts a set on me. "Notice I said nearly. There is a design flaw with the rod. If even a drop of water manages to get on it then it will short out."

Only seconds later the H.P.V. lands at the Constable base.

"Are you two ready?" the Oderian asks as he walks over to the button that will open the doors.

Nova and I nod, glancing at each other. We are as prepared for this as we could possibly be.

I squint as the doors open, letting in the bright light of the base. My eyes quickly adjust as I stare. I have never seen so many Constables in my life.

They mill around the large room, doing whatever their different jobs are. One walks up the ramp, eyeing Nova and me quickly before turning to the Oderian.

"What are they here for?" he asks, almost uninterested.

"We caught them snooping around the perimeter. We brought them in to make sure they weren't trying to gather intel for the rebels, sir," the Oderian tells him.

The Constable nods, "Very well. Take them to their cells. However, I will be coming by to interrogate them later. Every piece of information we can get on the rebels helps us farther along in ending this rebellion."

The Oderian takes my arm in one hand and Nova's arm in the other hand. He leads us along, occasionally giving one of us a good tug on the arm to not look too suspicious.

It takes much longer than I thought to get to the cells on the other side of the building. The base seems to be like a maze. I have no idea how we are going to navigate it to escape. The rebels may have sent us into a death trap because I fear sooner or later someone will recognize me or Nova and it will jeopardize the mission. I try to keep track of the twists and turns we take, but I soon lose count.

Finally, we stop in front of a heavy metal door. The door automatically opens for the agent, and we walk in. Thick cell doors line the walls. I jump slightly as I hear thumps and grunts of pain.

Suddenly a high-pitched scream pierces the air. It stops as suddenly as it started. I glance over at Nova who doesn't seem to have any problems with the unsettling noises. He is probably used to that sort of thing. It could have easily been something he heard every day as a Constable.

The agent shoves us into our cells and whispers, "The other prisoners have already been informed of your arrival. I will be back soon with a map of the base."

He shuts the door and it locks. I look around at the dimly lit room. "At least it's decently clean," I sigh.

Nova slides down the wall on the other side of the room, "They tend to clean them after each prisoner, so you aren't sitting in a pool of another's blood."

"Wonderful," I groan as I slide down the wall opposite him.

He glances up at me from the floor, "Prepare yourself for when the Constable comes in to interrogate us. They will not refrain from using force. I assume they will also pick on you first because it is procedure for them to break the weakest link if they catch more than one person. They have more work to do otherwise."

I nod, another wonderful thing to add to my list of great things that are happening today.

Nova and I sit in silence for a while, words coming to neither of us to make this situation any better than it previously was.

I can assume he is plotting our escape as we sit here, but even though I know him, it is still a mystery as to what is happening inside his head.

I jump slightly when I hear the door unlock. After what seemed like forever of nothing but silence, even the slightest noise can put me on edge.

The door slides open and the Constable from earlier appears. He glares down at the two of us. "Look at our two little spies."

Nova huffs and rolls his eyes. I know he's trying to draw attention away from me. However, the Constable doesn't take the bait. He glances over at Nova for a moment. I see a flicker of recognition in his eyes.

"If it isn't the infamous Nova Stargazer," the Constable sighs. "You know, I believe I remember seeing something sent out from the Council about you and the girl. I think it said you two broke into a small base and are currently the number one enemies of the Council," he says as he leans against the door, folding his muscular arms over his chest.

I internally groan, exactly what we need. The Council gunning for us more than they already were.

"I already sent a message to the Council, telling them that we have both of you in custody and we are prepared to interrogate you to find out information about the rebels." The Constable stands up and slowly walks towards me, eyeing me up and down.

"A hybrid, hmm? I thought your kind were nonexistent now," he laughs as he kneels down next to me.

"I'm here aren't I?" I sneer at him. I really don't feel like dealing with this Constable today.

He immediately stands back up and turns toward Nova. "I think today will be the day Nova Stargazer is finally broken."

"You won't break me, you should know better than to assume things like that," Nova responds as he stands up straighter, puffing out his chest in an attempt to look more menacing.

"I think otherwise. You see Stargazer, you have been out of the force for too long. There is new technology you have never seen, that you haven't been able to experience. For example..." the Constable pulls out something shaped like a small box. "This will show us some of your worst nightmares."

The Constable points the box at Nova, and it scans him. The Constable then sets the box down, and it produces an image.

Everything is blurry at first, but then the image comes into focus. I swear my hearts skip a beat when I see myself lying limp and bleeding in Nova's arms. Nova holds my body close as his own trembles with sobs. He rocks back and forth, unable to stem the tears that drip from his face onto my deathly still body. He desperately tries to stop the bleeding, applying pressure to the wound, but the blood still flows. It covers his hands and arms, the puddle he sits in quickly growing larger.

"Oh Nova," I breathe.

Suddenly it changes, and I see Nova standing there surrounded by bodies. It takes me a moment before I realize they are the bodies of dead rebels. I scan the bodies, finding Pandra among them. In his hand he holds a staff, dripping with blood. As his chest heaves with heavy breathing, his eyes are clouded with the distant look on his face.

Then, the image changes again. Once again, I see myself, however, I am pushed against a wall with someone's hand around my neck. I claw at the hand trying to get a single gulp of air. My hands fall to my sides as my eyes roll back into my head, and I go limp in the image.

I trace my eyes along. Looking to find out who is choking me to death in the image, I follow the fingers, arm, shoulder, neck, face. Nova.

The image abruptly disappears, and I find that Nova has smashed the small box. It sits on the floor in pieces. Nova doesn't look at me, avoiding my eyes.

The Constable laughs, "I see many reasons for her to be afraid of you."

"Those weren't real," Nova shakes his head.

"Oh, those were very real. They were taken straight from your own mind," the Constable grins.

I quickly realize what the Constable is trying to do. He is trying to make Nova mad, make Nova lash out so he would have a reason to take him on.

"They are not real," Nova repeats, his hands balling into fists.

"You didn't want her to know, did you? You didn't want her to know how much of a monster you really are," the Constable laughs.

Suddenly, Nova slams the Constable against the wall,

exactly as I was in the image.

"Don't you ever call me a monster," Nova sneers.

The Constable pulls back and his fist connects with Nova's jaw. Nova stumbles away, still avoiding my gaze. Before Nova could turn back around the Constable made it to me. He grabs me by the arm and yanks me to my feet.

"Another step and I'll snap her neck," he threatens as he wraps his arm around my neck.

Nova immediately calms down as I struggle to get out of the Constable's grip.

"Now sit down," the Constable commands.

Nova hesitates and the Constable tightens his grip on me.

"It's okay, I'll be fine. This filthy Constable won't kill me. I'll still be here," I gasp, the Constable now squeezing so tightly I can barely breathe.

"Not for much longer if you keep talking to me with that tone," he threatens. Nova sits down and the Constable's grasp loosens slightly.

I move without thinking, slipping myself out of his arms. My hand automatically goes to his shirt, and I wrap it around my fist, bringing him close to my face. "I'm going to talk to a murderer however I like. They don't deserve to be treated with respect," I hiss, then let go and shove him away from me.

He lands on his back, knocking the air out of his chest. He lays there for a moment, gasping for breath before he finally gets up smirking. "I do like 'em to start out feisty. Let's see how long it takes to break you." His hand connects with the side of my head, and I find myself splayed out on the floor, blinking away the black spots in my vision.

"Hey," Nova exclaims, jumping up from his seated position. The Constable stumbles back with the force behind the punch Nova threw at him.

"Violent aren't you Stargazer?" the Constable smiles and spits blood on the floor. "I know how long you can stand in an uneven fight, but let's see how she fairs in one." He pulls out a short metal rod.

Nova seems to recognize what it is within a glance. Suddenly, he pounces at the Constable, trying to disarm him of the object. Nova lets out a loud groan as the rod is jammed into his stomach. He collapses on the floor, unmoving except for the slight rise and fall of his chest and the blinking of his eyes.

"What did you do to him?" I exclaim as I scurry over to his still form.

The Constable laughs as he picks at the tip of the rod, "I gave him temporary paralysis."

I glared up at him as I slowly stand, "You monstrous son of a..."

"Oh dear, we can't have that type of language," he gasps in mock hurt. "Now, you will tell me what I want to know or else you will get more than temporary paralysis."

"Do what you like to me," I spit, "I'm not going to tell you a thing."

"I know that without a weapon you are defenseless, even with a weapon what chance would you have against me?" the Constable asks as he takes several steps toward me.

"More of a chance than you think," I growl and shove him back.

"I can't wait to watch you hang. No, wait, I think they will come up with a special way to die, seeing as how you are the last free hybrid. Oh, dear me you aren't free anymore," he smirks. "As for Lieutenant Stargazer here, he will be publicly executed for betraying the Council and undermining the authority of the Council Constables."

As I hear this, I snap. I am sick of hearing about how terrible it is going to be for us. The Council knows nothing, and they never will. I charge at the Constable, but he pins me to the wall beside him. A rise was what he wanted to get out of me.

I gasp for breath, his hand pressing into my throat and cutting off my airway. My fingers wrap around his wrist, trying to pull him away, but he is much stronger than me. I glance at Nova who is still unable to move.

The Constable pulls away slowly but jams his fist into my side several times. I hear a loud crack, and I scream in pain. I believe he may have broken several of my ribs. I slide down the wall once he lets go.

"I'll be back later," he sneers, standing over me, then turns and leaves.

My breaths are shallow, and it hurts horribly to even suck in a small bit of air. With one hand I pull myself to the floor and lay down.

I hear Nova grunt in pain then the slight rustle of his cloak as his paralysis wears off and he is able to move again. His face appears in my line of vision. "Are you alright?" he asks, kneeling down next to me.

I glare up at him. "No," I wince. "I think he broke one of my ribs...Maybe several."

Nova nods, "I need to see where." He fingers lightly press down my sides. I yelp in pain once he hits a spot on my mid left side. "At least it's low enough that it won't puncture anything vital."

"I heard a crack," I breathe.

"So did I," he glances up at my face.

"It hurts," my voice falters, the pain starting to really get to me. A few tears leak from the corners of my eyes, breaking my act of being strong.

Nova nods, silently brushing away my tears. He gently slides an arm underneath me and lifts my upper body, cradling me in his warm embrace.

"It hurts so much, Nova. Make it stop, Nova. Please make it stop. Make it all go away." With every shuddering breath I take, the pain seems to intensify. I have never felt this much pain. "Please Nova, please make it stop."

"I know, I know," he whispers, his hand slipping some of my stray hair behind an ear.

I squeeze my eyes shut, no matter what I do it doesn't seem to give me a break. The tears grow heavier and my airways seem to close with sobs.

"Hey, Ara?" Nova asks softly as he strokes my cheek trying to calm me.

"W-what?" I stutter through my sobs.

"I have a great idea. Would you like to hear it?" he says in a calming voice.

I nod, unable to get in a word between my sobs.

"When all this is done I think we should go exploring. We can venture around Ode o-or we could be the first Oderians to leave the planet and explore like the humans did. We could go to other planets and meet the people who live there," he explains as he continues to brush his fingers against my cheek.

"Could we see stars no one has ever seen before and create new constellations to teach people about?" I ask, trying to stop crying and suppress the pain.

He nods, "Of course. We can go wherever you want to go. All you have to do is survive this. Can you do that for me, get through this and the war? Then we can go wherever you want to go."

"I can do that." I try to take a deep breath but wince in pain. "It hurts so badly."

"I know, and I'm sorry I can't do much about it here. You are going to have to bear with it until we get back to base. Rest for now, he will be back before you know it. You will have trouble sleeping in so much pain, so I want you to at least try; we've done a lot today. Close your eyes and relax. Imagine we are exploring, going anywhere you want. Close your eyes and everything will be fine, I promise."

I take a deep breath. Black spots appear then take over.

Chapter Eighteen

In the Council Dwellings

Zubenelgenubi sits upon his 'throne' with the rest of the Council at his feet.

"You have displeased me. I requested that the two rebels be found and brought in. Why has this not been done?" he sneers down at them.

"W-we have been trying. They have proved...difficult to be found. They seem to appear then disappear on the radars, sir," one Council member stutters.

Suddenly, the doors to the hall fly open. "Brother," the Oderian exclaims.

The Council members look from this new Oderian to their leader, in awe at the striking resemblance before them.

"Oh, what is it Zubeneschamali?" the Council leader sighs.

"The two fugitives. They have been apprehended, and are being held at base four fifty-two," Zubeneschamali gasps, quickly catching his breath.

"Who is this? We demand to know why he is in the Council dwellings," a member exclaims, still slightly bewildered at the sight.

Zubenelgenubi motions to his look-alike, "This is my brother and fellow leader of the Council. He preferred to stay in hiding...until now I'm assuming."

Zubeneschamali nods, "We have very important matters to discuss."

His brother nods and stands.

"What fate is to befall the two fugitives?" a female Council member asks, halting the brothers. "Shouldn't we all have a say in what is to happen to the two rebels?"

"You will have no say in the matter," Zubenelgenubi waves her off.

"We are the Council," she protests.

The two brothers turn to her, glaring down their noses, obviously displeased at the objections. "You have no say," Zubeneschamali exclaims. His brother nods and with a swish of their long black cloaks they turn to leave, their fading footsteps echoing across the hall.

"How much have you found out?" Zubenelgenubi asks once they are alone.

"They were brought in for trespassing around the perimeter of the base. However, I fear that is not the case. A team of Constables recently cut off a line of supplies to the rebels. What they found is being stored at that base along with many valuable prisoners," Zubeneschamali explains.

His brother nods. "They may be there to free the supplies and the prisoners. That would be a plot the rebels would enact. You say they also sent Stargazer with the girl?"

"They did indeed and that is what I fear. With him in that base, there is no telling what the rebels have instructed. He is very hard to crack. His companion, though, is not," Zubeneschamali sighs.

"They must be careful around the hybrid. He could have taught her things about the Constables that we must never let the rest of the planet know. A hybrid knowing information such as that could be potentially detrimental to our cause," Zubenelgenubi pauses, waiting for his brother to reply.

"I agree."

"We must hold them there and get what information we can out of the hybrid. There is no point in trying to pry anything out of Stargazer, it would waste what little time we have before this war is in full force. Every little piece of information can give us an advantage over the rebels," he finishes. "The hybrid's father is also being held at that base. I planned to break her by having her watch him die."

Zubeneschamali nods, "I don't have a problem with that."

They stand in silence for a moment before Zubene schamali speaks again.

"There is also the possibility of using them against their own side. The hybrid can easily be used as bait for the rebels. They will not risk completely destroying the hybrid breed," he says.

"I understand where you are going but she is the wrong one to use. We must use Stargazer," his brother shakes his head.

"How could we get him to betray his own side?" Zubeneschamali asks.

"Does he have a trigger?" Zubenelgenubi urges.

"Yes..." His brother trails off starting to see where the plan was heading.

"Then go get me General Vanil," Zubenelgenubi exclaims.

His brother races out of the room in search of the General.

Chapter Nineteen

Ara

I groan, slowly opening my eyes. My ribs throb. At least Oderians heal quickly, and I won't have to worry about this for too long.

"How do you feel?" Nova asks from the other side of the room.

I glare at him, slowly sitting up. "What do you think?"

Nova shrugs, "I thought I would ask." He looks back down at the map the agent must have given him while I was out.

I lean against the wall, "Have you figured out how to get us out of here yet?"

"I'm working on it. The agent will let us out of our cell. However, it will be up to us to get the others out. He gave me the silver we need to fake your death. In fact, I told him the Constable had broken your ribs. Anyone we run into that sees you alive we will have to kill because they all think you are dead. It will save you from actually trying to fake your own death." Nova explains.

"Wonderful," I sigh.

"So, when the Constable comes back you need to be dead," he instructs. "After that, we will begin the plan."

I jump when I hear the door unlock. Nova looks to me.

"Quickly, lay back down. Close your eyes. Stay silent. Breathe as little as possible," he exclaims in a whisper.

I do as he says as the door starts to open.

"Maaz?" Nova gasps.

My eyes shoot open. Maaz is my father's name. I push myself up with one hand, wincing in pain and holding my side with

114

my other hand. My breath catches in my throat as my eyes fall on the frail form of my father. The wrinkles on his face seem deeper and he looks moons older than he actually is now.

"Ara, you are still alive," My father breathes.

The same Constable who broke my ribs gives us a mischievous grin, holding my father's arm in an iron grip.

My father turns to Nova, who sits in awe. "You've done your job better than I hoped, Nova. You have kept her alive through all this."

Nova nods, "I would do anything for her. You know that."

The Constable sighs. "This has been a wonderful reunion and all but I kind of have orders directly from Zubenelgenubi himself that I have to carry out. No excuses."

I look to Nova in a panic then look back at the Constable. "What orders?"

"To kill him," the Constable shrugs, motioning to my father.

"What? No. You can't do that," I exclaim, trying to stand up.

"Ara. Ara, stop," Nova says, trying to stop me from standing up.

"I am not going to let that idiotic Constable kill my father."

"Ara, calm down. It will be alright. Don't worry about me. I am old. I have served my purpose here on Ode. I have seen you one last time. There is nothing left for me," my father explains with sad eyes.

"No. You aren't allowed to say things like that. I need you." I try to stand again but my legs give out underneath me, and I collapse back down on the floor. I try once again but fail, my weak body falling to the floor.

"You will be fine Ara. You still have Nova," my father says, as the Constable draws his staff, clearly amused by the scene playing out in front of him.

"Help me, Nova," I cry. He sits there for a moment. "Help me. Please." Tears prick at my eyes in frustration.

He finally gives in, leaning down and whispering in my ear as he helps me stand, "I know you don't want to think about things like this right now, but after that Constable kills your father, you need to pretend to die. I don't care how you do it, but you have to do it no matter what."

I shudder in pain, leaning on Nova for support. My lip quivers as tears slide down my face.

My father meets my gaze. "You've made me proud Ara. Don't give up, you will end this war."

"Please don't. Please don't do this," I beg the Constable.

The Constable breaks the globe on the top of his staff and runs my father through with it all in one movement.

"No!" I scream. Nova holds me back as my father crumples to the floor.

"Remember Ara..." My father chokes, coughing up blood as he bleeds out. "I trusted Nova for a reason...Give him what he wants, it's not that much..." he wheezes.

I fight against Nova. "Let go of me," I screech. "I have to save him."

"End this war for me, Ara." My father's gaze turns to Nova. "Take good care of her Nova..." His eyes roll up into his head as he breathes his last breath. A single silver tear drips from each eye.

I turn away from the sight sobbing against Nova's chest. He wraps his arms around me, trying to comfort me. I pull away, stumbling to the body of my father, and fall to my knees.

I glance back at Nova, the look in his eyes telling me I have to fake my own death now. I bite my lip, tears still running down my cheeks. This is going to be gross.

I position myself with my back to the Constable. Still sobbing, I scream at the top of my lungs, rocking back and forth as I do so. I place my hand in the puddle of my father's blood.

I keep sobbing while pressing the bloody hand to my lips, pretending to cough as I turn around. I wince in pain, this isn't doing any good for my ribs.

"Ara?" Nova asks, taking a step forward.

I pull my hand from my face, revealing the blood around my mouth and covering my hand, looking as if I had coughed it all up.

"Ara, no." Nova comes to my side quickly.

The Constable stands there, eyes wide.

"What's happening?" I act, looking down to my bloody hand.

"Y-your ribs must have punctured your lungs," Nova

stutters.

I pretend to cough again, this time harder. I double over, wheezing, acting like I can't get enough air.

"Ara, breathe," Nova glances at the Constable. "You did this to her. She is going to die now."

I lower myself all the way to the floor as the Constable responds, "What did I do?"

"You broke her ribs. It's your fault," Nova exclaims, pulling me into his arms.

I start coughing again; I have to make this look as real as possible.

"N-Nova..." I gasp.

He holds me tight, "Stay with me, Ara. You can't leave me yet."

"What's happening?" the Constable asks, stepping forward.

Nova throws his hand out, "Stay back. You did this. If it weren't for you, she would be fine."

The Constable takes several steps back, not wanting to make Nova any more up upset. He should know how mad Nova will pretend to be after this.

I shake my head, coughing again. "I can't do this...anymore."

"Do what?" Nova asks, stroking my cheek.

"Be here, without any family," I cough, tears running down my cheeks again.

"Don't you dare do this to me, Ara. Don't you dare," Nova threatens.

"I can't," I gasp, taking Nova's hand from my face and holding it for a moment before going limp.

"No. No. Ara," Nova exclaims, shaking me as if trying to wake me up.

"Is she dead?" the Constable asks.

"I said, stay back," Nova snaps. "Ara...please, No." After a moment Nova gives up. "She's dead."

"How?" I hear the Constable take several steps towards Nova and me.

"Oh, I don't know, you broke her ribs and killed her father?" Nova sets me down, sarcasm lining his voice, "I have no idea."

"She is really dead?"

"Yes! She is dead! Will you stop rubbing it in?" Nova snaps.

"Where's the silver?" the Constable presses.

I imagine that Nova pulled the vial with the silver from his cloak, "If you want absolute proof. Here. That is all I have left of her. Lose it and I will kill you myself."

"How could you have let this happen?" the Constable exclaims.

"How could I? I couldn't do anything to stop you. Did you forget I was stuck in temporary paralysis? This is all on you. The Council is not going to be pleased that you killed their one way to get information about the rebels," Nova says coldly.

"You knew this would happen, didn't you?" The Constable's steps echo as he gets closer to Nova.

"How was I to know she would die? It wasn't me who killed her anyway. Ah, think of the things the Council is going to do to you once they learn that you killed the last hybrid." I hear the rustle of Nova's cloak as he moves. "Now leave, there is nothing left here for you to get. All the information you might have been able to use has died with her. Remember, it's your fault."

The Constable huffs, and turns leaving the room with the realization Nova was correct.

I sit up once the door is closed, "Good job there. I really think he's mad now."

Nova shakes his head. "I'm surprised that actually worked. The agent should be by and unlock the door soon. Will you be able to walk?"

"Maybe?" I answer, unsure if I could even stand.

I pull myself up the wall, standing wobbly on my own two feet, I glance at Nova.

He nods, "Good."

I look at the body of my father, shaking my head. "I don't understand why he had to die, or why I had to watch as he was murdered."

Nova places a hand on my shoulder, "Zubenelgenubi and

the Council are trying to get under your skin. They are trying to mess with your head, get you to make a mistake. Your father was dead long before now. You know that. What you saw today was your father being freed from a shell he had been trapped in. Don't feel bad, it wasn't your fault, there was nothing you could do."

"I know," I sigh, trying to pull my gaze away from my father's body.

"We can't dwell on it because we have to focus on this mission, or else you really will end up dead," Nova says, turning me away from the bloody scene. He glances at my face. "You look like you ripped someone apart with all that blood on your face."

I shrug, "I guess I'm really going to scare some people."

Nova's head snaps toward the door as it is unlocked. "He said he would leave the passcodes to all the cells outside the door. Let's go."

Nova slowly opens the door and finds a small tablet. He picks it up and turns it on, scrolling through the passcodes. He looks to me, "We can free everyone now."

We quickly locate the control panel and punch in the passcodes. We hear the doors unlock one by one. Nova then goes down the hall opening the doors. The prisoners file out a few at a time. They all seem to realize the plan the agent told them about is now in action.

Nova leads us with the map. I follow behind him and the freed prisoners follow quietly behind me. Once again, the base is like a maze. I quickly lose track of the twists and turns, but Nova seems to guide us with ease.

I keep up as best I can. My ribs throb with each breath I take. The fake coughing earlier didn't help me any, but at least I will be healed soon. Possibly a moon or so and I should be back to normal. I'm glad Oderians heal quicker than humans do.

Suddenly Nova puts his hand up, signaling for everyone behind him to stop. He pauses listening for something. I hear what he does, footsteps coming down the hall. "Stay back and let me handle this," he whispers to me.

I nod. I know I am in no shape to be fighting right now, besides we don't want to ruin the illusion of my death. The rest of the prisoners and I back a little way down the hall. Depending on how many there are, this could get ugly. I peek around the corner I hide behind.

The second the Constables have rounded the corner down the hall, Nova is on them. Quickly disarming one, Nova uses the Constable's own weapon against him. He shatters the glass globe and the Constable falls to the floor, a pool of purple blood surrounding him. The other has enough time to draw his staff, making the fight against Nova on slightly more even ground.

They stare at each other for a moment as if daring their opponent to strike first. The Constable makes the first move, running at Nova, but he uses the same technique he used while training me. Nova diverts the Constable's momentum and sends him slamming into the wall. I flinch at the sound of Nova running him through with the staff. The staff crunches as it goes right through bone then hits the wall with a thud.

Nova turns back to us, his chest heaving with the effort he put into killing the two Constables. He motions for us to follow, and we continue our way down the brightly lit halls.

"We're almost to the other side of the building where the supplies are being held," he calls back to us after a few more twists and turns.

Moments later we enter a large hanger, the same one I believe we came in through. However, it seems the Constables had been waiting for us. No wonder why we saw so few in the hall on the way out. They were all here waiting for us, prepared to cut us down.

I glance back at some of the former prisoners, some have been badly beaten while others look like they could stand their ground in a fight, and even if they can't they are going to have to now. I hope that I have had enough training from Nova to stand a chance.

"Ara, catch," Nova throws the staff he had stolen back to me. "You're going to have to lead this one. I'll be right back. I think I saw where they stored our weapons. I'm going to get them back while you take care of them."

Nova disappears through another door. The former prisoners look to me. I am not equipped to be leading a group of people, but I'm going to have to.

"Um..." I trail off quietly.

Nova is so much better at this kind of thing, I have no experience in telling people what to do so they don't get killed. The Constables haven't noticed our arrival yet, seeing as how we are hiding behind a stack of supplies.

"Those who are able to need to fight with me. The rest of you need to start loading the supplies into the H.P.V.'s so as soon as we are ready we can take off." Since they seem to understand, I continue, "Let's go."

I stand up from behind the supplies and face the Constables. They don't seem to notice us. They are too transfixed on the door they thought we would use to get in.

They're all going to die, so it doesn't matter if I draw attention to myself. "Hey," I yell. They jolt toward me at the sound of my voice. "I'm a hybrid and a rebel, come and get me," I could have come up with something much better but oh well. We don't have time for things like that right now.

The prisoners behind me stand up and rush out toward them as insanity ensues. Some take-up supplies in their arms and make a beeline for the H.P.V.s, others going head on into the battle.

I make my way slowly, using the techniques Nova taught me for quick kills. Those skills seem to be useful in a situation such as this. I hear a Constable come up behind me. I whip around, jabbing the staff's broken globe into the Constable's stomach. He falls to the ground and I turn back around slashing at another Constable.

I'm surprised I have lasted this long. Within no time the freed prisoners and I stand surrounded by the majority of the Constable force from this base. My chest heaves, and I wince in pain with every breath.

I turn around and find all the supplies had been loaded onto the H.P.V.s during the battle. As one human comes up to me, I ask, "How many did we lose?"

"Three," he answers.

"Fewer than I thought we would, that's good. Now, Nova should be back soon. We should be under way before any reinforcements get here," I tell him. I turn back to the rest of the group, "Go ahead and load the H.P.V.s. The less that still need to board them when Nova arrives, the quicker we can go." I groan in pain as the adrenaline starts to wear off. I guess I was so caught up in the fight I didn't feel any pain, but I sure do now.

One by one, I watch the group get smaller as they load. Suddenly, I feel a hand on my shoulder. I glance back and see Nova with our staffs slung across his back.

"How many?" he asks quietly as he hands me my staff.

"Only three," I answer, placing my staff and its sling where it belongs across my back.

He nods, "We had well-trained people then. That or the Constables here are poorly trained."

We follow the last of the group onto the H.P.V.'s. "Everything is loaded so we should be able to make it back to base without running into too many problems," I tell him as I sit down, wincing slightly.

"The agent said there would already be pilots, let's take off." Nova knocks on the door to the control room and the H.P.V. comes to life beneath us. "What is a two-day journey on foot shouldn't take us nearly as long in one of these. We will be back to base soon."

As we fly back we tend as best we can to the wounded. Many have minor cuts and bruises. However, there are a few that will need major treatment back at base. The best we can do here is keep the humans from bleeding to death and the Oderians from falling into regenerative shock.

We arrive back at base quicker than I thought we would. The wounded are rushed into care. The supplies are unloaded and sorted out to fit the sizes of the rations the rebels provide. A tall young human meets us outside the H.P.V. "Messier would like to debrief both of you," he says.

Nova and I follow him back to the same room in which we were given the mission. Messier sits casually in a chair but stands up as we enter. "You two have done a fine job, very fine job." He says and sits back down. "Please sit, but I'm afraid I'm going to have to cut the celebration short."

"Why? What's happened?" I ask as I sit down in a chair across from him with Nova at my side.

"I have gotten word from some undercover agents that the Council has put a target on your backs. However, I was also told they believe you are dead, Ara. How would they come up with such a thing?" Messier asks coldly.

"We faked my death," I answer honestly. "We figured it would be better if the last free hybrid was assumed to be dead by the Council. It would take the target you were speaking of off my back. Besides, I don't think the Council knows about Pandra."

He nods. "It was a good idea. However, it does not erase the target that is on Nova's back."

Nova shrugs. "There has always been a target on my back. How could this be any different?"

"They want you dead or working for them," Messier shakes his head. "You will have to be extra careful on missions. However, there will not need to be many more. We are almost ready to attack. That's all I have for you two right now, go get rest and heal those broken ribs," he dismisses us.

I stand and make my way back to my room and collapse into the regeneration tube.

Chapter Twenty

Ara

I groan. My chest aches with each breath I take. Why did the Constable have to break my ribs? It really wasn't necessary for his cause.

The Constables. My eyes shoot open, and I sit up but end up hitting my head on the glass above me.

"Ow," I yelp. I reach up and open the glass of the regeneration tube. I slowly glance around the room. Everything is so different here than it was at home. No war, no Constables, I didn't have to worry about if I was about to be murdered or put into temporary paralysis. Nope, everything was normal.

My mind floats back to the image of my father. The staff protruding from his abdomen. The look on his face as he collapsed and bled out on the floor in front of me. I don't know if I will ever be able to forget that image. *How could the Council do something like that? How could Zubenelgenubi do that? How could he plan to have my father killed before my eyes?* I thought Constables were monsters because they kill for fun, for sport. No, Zubenelgenubi is the monster for tearing apart families. One day, I will make him pay for what he has done. He will pay for everyone he has killed, everyone he hurt, every single family he tore to pieces.

I pull my thoughts away from him. I think about home again. The calmness I felt when I was home. I try to imagine myself there now, in the comfort of my room, prepared to have a normal day with the people I know and love. The people, who are now probably dead, made me who I am...or rather who I was. I'm not the same person I was when I lived on my own.

Suddenly, I hear the door open and close and I shut my eyes, imagining that it was the door to my room and Nova was coming in to say good morning. We would exchange a few words in greeting, make a few jokes and laugh together. He would then leave my room, waiting outside the door for me, still joking around and laughing. I would change into my Tan Dew and we would go on a run, exactly like the day everything started. The day my entire world fell apart and was ripped apart by none other than the Council and Zubenelgenubi.

A hand touches my shoulder and I flinch. I didn't even hear the person walk over to me. My body moves before I could even register the movement. My eyes shoot open and without so much as glancing at the person's face, I jump out of the tube and pull the person into a tight choke hold. Nova taught me some defensive moves back a few moons ago while we were training. He told me he thought I would need them for self-defense in case I ever found myself in a sticky situation without a staff or any other weapon.

"Ara let go," the person gasps, clawing at my arms desperate for a gulp of air.

I realize who it is by their voice. I immediately let go.

"Sorry, Nova," I say softly, rubbing my temples as I sit down on the edge of my regeneration tube, "You startled me."

"It's okay. I probably should have knocked before I entered the room. I came in here to check on you, to see how you and your broken ribs are doing. Clearly, though you are on edge," Nova says, as he rubs his neck.

"What do you expect? I was imprisoned for a day, almost beaten to death. I watched my father get run through by a Constable then bleed to death. Being on edge is a bit of an understatement," I reply.

Glancing around the room, I sigh. This place will never be my home, no matter how much I imagine and dream that it is.

"What happened?" I ask as I study Nova. He has a few bruises on his face I hadn't seen yesterday when we arrived back at base.

"What these?" he asks, motioning to the bruises. "I kicked a few Constable's hind ends while trying to get our staffs back. They gave me quite the beating. That is, once I managed to grab a staff they didn't last much longer. A good thing too, from what I have been hearing, we left in barely enough time. The reinforcements arrived there not long after we left. We all would have been goners if we had stayed," Nova explains. "I bet Zubenelgenubi was pissed about how that Constable killed you. Someone is going to die because he didn't get to kill you himself."

"So, what do you need, other than checking on me?" I question.

"Messier requested he see us immediately," Nova says.

I knew he had ulterior motives for coming in here. It is never to make sure I'm alright or to talk. There is always something happening I need to see, or someone always wants to talk to me.

"Alright," I sigh, "So did he say why?"

"No," he shakes his head. "Let's go. It's better if he tells you in person. It's not really my place to say anything else." Nova beckons me to follow him and walks out of the room.

We go down several hallways and through several doors, then we come to a small room with a hologram table in the center and some humans and Oderians gathered around it. Pandra leans against the wall of the room picking at her fingertips.

"If the Constables really are here, then we will have to call for reinforcements from the secondary base because we don't have enough people here to defend against them," a man says as he points to places on the table, then looks up.

"Ahh, Nova you have come back to join us," Messier says.

"What do you need?" Nova asks as he walks up to join the men at the table.

Pandra looks up from the other side of the room, running over to me as soon as she sees me come through the door, "Ara, you're alive."

"Yes, I am alive," I sigh, not really in the mood to deal with Pandra's craziness at the moment.

"We all thought you were dead after we intercepted a message from the Constable base about how you were killed! I thought I was the last hybrid left alive," she exclaims, wrapping an arm around my shoulder.

"It wasn't real. We faked my death to get the Council and Zubenelgenubi off my back. They were breathing down my neck there for a while." I smile at her politely, as I remove her arm from my shoulder.

Pandra is a wonderful hybrid, but she is a little bit too affectionate for my taste. It's one of the things I share with Nova, other people touching me is not really my favorite thing on the planet.

"I hope you are feeling better Ara?" Messier asks as he turns to me, pulling me from my thoughts.

I nod. "I'm fine."

"I'm sorry to call you in on such short notice and to interrupt your conversation with Pandra, but I must speak with you." Messier turns back to the table as if to tell me I need to look at it too.

I glance at Nova, confused. What is so urgent? Why have we been called here at such short notice? It can't be another mission. "Okay," I nod. "Why exactly are we here?"

Nova pulls me toward the table and everyone stares at me either like they've seen a ghost or in amazement.

"What?" I ask, even more confused.

Nova looks at me. "Ignore them, like Pandra, they still thought you were dead until you walked in the room. They were all taken a bit off guard."

"Hi, I'm alive," I choke out trying desperately not to laugh. I can't imagine seeing someone you thought was dead walk into a room alive and healthy like nothing ever happened. I'm surprised Pandra handled it as she did. I would have thought the second I walked in she would have tackled me to the ground for making her think I was dead.

Nova turns to Messier, "I haven't said anything to Ara yet. I didn't think it was my place to explain. Go ahead, the quicker she knows, the faster we can prepare."

"The Council is holding what is left of the hybrids in the dwellings and they are going to have one last public execution," he says. "They will also execute humans and Oderians who had hybrid children and associated with them.

Suddenly, my throat feels like it is closing up. A lot of people are about to die by both the Council's and Zubenelgenubi's hands.

"So, what are we going to do about it?" I ask.

Messier looks at me and shakes his head. "There is not much we can do other than fight this war. We have no forces to spare to go out on a rescue mission. There is also no telling how many we will have left from the battles which will have occurred between now and before the execution is to take place."

I turn away, frustrated. My parents are both already dead, all my friends and everyone I grew up around are going to die, everyone except Nova. He's all I have left.

I feel him softly rest his hand on my shoulder. "We will find a way. We always do."

His sparkling silver eyes stare into mine as I glance up at him. "Promise me you will never leave like they did?" I ask in a whisper so quiet that I could barely hear it. He knows exactly who I am referring to. I can't lose him like I lost my parents.

He smiles down at me solemnly and replies, "Never."

Suddenly someone clears their throat and says, "Sorry to interrupt this beautiful moment, but we have to plan out a war here." Nova looks away and nods, but his hand doesn't leave my shoulder.

At the moment the one thing holding me together and keeping me from exploding on the rebels for not trying to save all those people is Nova. I feel guilty for pushing him away not that long ago even though we are on better terms now. Guilt like that lingers. I don't know if I will ever be able to forgive myself for putting him through all that pain.

Chapter Twenty-one

Ara

Several Moons later

"How was that, Nova?" I ask as I turn to him, still holding my staff in an offensive position.

"You have always learned very quickly and in the past few moons you have become very good," Nova grins.

Between all the missions and everything that had been happening Nova and I haven't had very much time to train. However, because we faked my death the rebels have not sent us out on any more missions. This has given us the past several moons off and enough time for Nova to finish training me, in case a situation like what happened at the Constable base on our last mission ever repeats itself.

"Do you think I will be able to take on Constables on my own?" I ask him.

"You might, it depends on the situation. You become easily distracted by your emotions. If you let that continue you will start making mistakes," Nova answers, leaning against a practice dummy.

"How do you keep yourself from getting distracted?"

"I put myself somewhere else, I pretend like I'm training, like I'm battling a practice dummy," he shrugs, picking at the coarse fabric that covers the one he is leaning against.

"That's why your eyes get clouded and distant. It's hard to bring you back because you enjoy training like we are now. You enjoy it so much you want every battle to be like training." I nod, starting to understand why.

If every battle is training then the stakes are lower, lessening the stress. If there is less stress, stress is not a distraction and it will be harder to make mistakes. Maybe I'll try that method. It wouldn't hurt, anything that might help me stay alive, I will try.

I relax, catching my breath when the doors to the training center fly open. I recognize one of the humans I saw in the many meetings Nova and I have been to over the past few moons to figure out what the rebels will do next. He stands there, chest heaving and looking around desperately. Nova runs over to the young man and I follow behind him.

The man doesn't look good. He is in a panic and has a wound to his head. It bleeds ferociously, running down his face and dripping to the floor.

"What is it? What's wrong? Has something happened?" Nova asks quickly.

"C-Constables. They've found us. Th-they're looking for you," the man gasps, pointing to me then collapsing, probably passing out from fear and blood loss.

"Classic human," Nova mutters, then turns to me, "Ara I…"

"No, I will not sit here, letting you go out there and have all the fun," I interrupt.

The second I finish my sentence the entire building shakes and little pieces of the ceiling rain down on us in dust and pebbles. Nova glares at me, "You aren't ready yet. I will not watch you get yourself killed."

"I will not sit here and watch people die for me. I'd much rather fight for myself. I have fought before. I killed as many Constables as everyone else did before we escaped from the Constable base on our last mission. So why do you want to keep me from fighting now? You know the rebels need every person they can get out there to help," I exclaim, glaring right back at Nova.

Nova shakes his head. "No, Ara," he yells, out of frustration. "I will not let you go out there."

I shrink back, Nova has never yelled at me like that. I have seen him like this before, mad at someone else, but he has never been this upset with me.

"Now, let's go." He snatches my wrist and pulls me out of

the training room.

"Nova," I shriek in pain as he grips my wrist too tightly, but it seems he wasn't paying attention. I drop my staff in my effort to pull my wrist from his hand. I push on his hand and pick at his fingers, trying to get him to let go.

He pulls me down a few halls and down a flight of stairs I never saw before. I thought I had explored the entire base during these last few moons when we didn't have a mission.

"Nova, let go," I cry out in pain, but still, he doesn't turn back to me. "Nova, stop." I try once again to pull my wrist out of his firm grip. I plant my feet on the floor, trying to get him to stop walking so fast and turn around to talk to me.

He suddenly whips around and growls, "What?" His eyes stare at me angrily.

"I-it hurts, let go, please," I stutter.

Something about this side of Nova scares me. The look in his eyes sends chills down my back. It scares me more than when I found out he used to be a Constable. He loosens his grip a little and without a word turns around and continues on. The building shakes again, and dust rains down from the ceiling as the lights flicker. The building groans, the walks creaking like it is under an immense amount of pressure. What is going on outside?

Then Nova stops in front of a large, heavy looking door and starts punching numbers into the keypad. "I want you to go in here and stay put. The Constables will not be able to get to you if you are in there." He straightens up and turns away from me. His voice suddenly soft, "Please, Ara."

His soft voice adds to my worry. If he is trying to hide me away inside some room Constables supposedly can't get into, clearly Nova is worried this will be the end of the rebels. He is worried it could be the beginning of a road that ends with me hanging dead on the steps of the Council dwellings with Zubenelgenubi laughing in the background.

"Nova," I say quietly, "Please don't leave me here." I set my hand on his shoulder, but he shakes me off, as I did to Pandra after we got back from our last mission.

"No, Ara, go hide," he whispers, trying to keep his voice level. "This is a war. This is not something to be taken lightly. If hiding means you live, that's what you must do."

"Nova, please don't leave me. You promised you wouldn't," I beg. "What about Pandra? Shouldn't she hide too?"

He whips around, "Sometimes I make promises I can't keep. Believe me, I don't want to leave you here either. I don't want to go up there and fight those Constables. Right now, I'd almost rather sit here and be a coward. I have to go up there and stand up for what I believe in, though. I believe in keeping you safe. Pandra is the least of my worries right now. Your father wanted me to keep you safe, not her."

I groan in frustration, "Why are you so keen on keeping me safe? Yes, I get it. I'm one of the last hybrids, but apparently, even my death won't end the war."

Nova stares at the ground and tugs on his hair. Something is up with him.

"Nova, what is it?" I ask cautiously.

He doesn't answer me.

"What is it, Nova? Don't you dare start keeping any more secrets from me."

"Why am I so keen on keeping you safe? Why? Because I'm in love with you," he exclaims. "I am in love with you, Ara."

I take a few steps back, surprised at his sudden outburst.

"I said it twice, is that enough or do I need to say it a third time?" He sighs as he stares at the ground. "That is why I am so keen on protecting you. It's not because your father entrusted your life into my hands, it's because I want to keep you safe. I don't want you to die. I don't think I could live with myself if I lost you because I allowed you to fight in a battle which may take your life. I cannot do it."

The building shakes again. The lights flicker and go out. The building continues to rumble. Suddenly there is a loud crash, and the ground vibrates as part of the building collapses somewhere.

"Nova?" I call out, not sure if the rest of the building is about to collapse or not.

"I'm right here," he replies from behind me.

"Why did the lights go out?" I ask in a whisper, listening for any indicators we are about to be crushed. The dark is thick, and no light is leaking from any cracks. It seems to weigh down on my shoulders.

"The Constables most likely destroyed the generators so we would have no power. I need to leave and go help the others," he says.

"No. Nova, please don't leave me here. What if the Constables come down here and find me? They can't know I'm still alive. It would put a target back on me," I plead as I turn in the direction of his voice.

"Ara," he sighs as he sets his hands on my shoulders gently. "If you go in that room and close the door, they won't be able to get to you. They will never even be able to guess the key code to open the door. Now, I have to go help the rebels. I am one of the few here that actually know a thing or two about the Constables."

Suddenly, there is a low rumble and the lights flicker back on. I find myself staring into the silver eyes of Nova. He smiles at me sadly and brushes a wisp of hair behind my ear. He hugs me tightly then letting go of me, holds me at arm's length.

"Stay here. I'll be back soon," he says. Before I could say anything, he turns and runs off, back the way we came.

I sigh deeply and kick at the wall, frustrated. He loves me? When did this happen?

After a while, it seemed like I had been standing there forever. I slowly slide down the wall as the building shakes. I wonder what is happening up there. The lights go out again and I hear loud footsteps coming down the hallway. I question myself, do I stay or do I run?

Chapter Twenty-two

Nova

It breaks my heart I had to leave her there all alone. Why did I have to be so cruel when we started to repair our friendship? Why did I have to grip her wrist so tightly? She was crying out for me to let go, and I was so wrapped up in keeping her safe from Constables I forgot to protect her from myself.

I can get extremely violent when I get angry because I use it as a defense mechanism, I remind myself. That's what Constables are trained to do, channel their anger at anything, everything, and use it to hurt innocent people.

I shake this thought out of my head and draw my staff as I open the door. What I see astounds me. I have never seen so many rebels in one place, and they are all fighting against the Constables. I guess I never saw the entire force all together, maybe groups here and there around the base, never all together. There were more than I had originally thought.

I scan the edge of the mass of rebels and Constables I see the Constables brought some artillery with them. Instead of using a staff, the traditional weapon of choice for an Oderian, the Constables are using hydro-guns.

I watch as the Constables shoot down rebels with the same stuff they use to power their H.P.V.s. The liquid flies across the battlefield, going right through several rebels. They fall to the ground holding their sides or legs in pain. The liquid eats away their Tan Dews and their flesh. It sizzles and bubbles with the most putrid smell.

Messier runs up to me, turning my attention from the terrible sight in front of me. He holds his side in pain. "Nova I don't know how much longer the base is going to hold, but I have called for reinforcements from the secondary base. They should be here soon, but I'm not going to live that long," he gasps as he removes his hands from his side.

His shirt is seared away and crusty along the edges, and his skin is dissolving away from both his side and his hands. Blood leaks from his wounds and stains the ground. He had been hit by a hydro gun. From the looks of the wound, it happened a while ago. He doesn't have very much longer left.

"N-Nova," he stutters, "I want you to lead the rebels to victory. Who better than an ex-constable to beat the Council and Zubenelgenubi at their own game." He falls to his knees. I kneel down next to him and help him lay back.

He whispers, "Keep that girl safe. She will be a key player in this game, and when it's all over settle down with her. She's good girl." With that he dies, the liquid still dissolving his body. Soon, there will be nothing left of Messier.

I stare at the ground for a moment before I stand up. Messier had a good heart and didn't deserve to die at the hands of a Constable, let alone a Constable using a hydro gun.

I stand up and look around. The base is on a decent sized hill, and I can see down into the valley where the rebels and the Constables are fighting. They should be able to hear me from here.

"Listen up," I yell at the top of my lungs. I have to say something, if there is anything I can do to help us win this war, I will do it.

Everyone's head snaps up, and the fighting stops. Both Constables and rebels stare up at me. I set the end of my staff on the ground and stand up straight. Rebels grin up at me, proud of their fellow soldier. Constables stare up at me in amazement, many of them have probably heard of but never saw me before in person.

"Who are we?" I ask looking around slowly. "Who are we to judge a person? To judge a person on their type of blood? Pure or tainted? Are they really that different? Do we have the right to judge them like that? Do we have the right to tear small children, infants from their homes? Do we have the right to throw those children, innocent children, into a prison?

Sentence them to death and make a party out of it? They're children. They can't control who their parents are or what type of blood they have. We, the rebels are trying to protect those innocent children and yet you Constables killed one of the last hybrid girls out there. You brutally murdered her because of the so-called impurity of her blood. She's dead but you still persist. She wouldn't have wanted anyone to die for her, yet many good men, women, human and Oderian have died here, one of which was the rebel leader himself. He died at the hands of a Constable using a hydro gun. In his last moments, he appointed me as the new leader. I refuse to let him or the hybrid you murdered die in vain, so I ask of you, to forget your differences. Stop this war before there is no one left to fight it." I finish my speech and the rebels clap and cheer.

"What if we don't?" a Constable yells angrily. "We know you are harboring others."

"You will die at the hands of a human," I reply with the ultimate dishonor to a Constable.

The second I finish the fighting starts again. There really is no way to end this war is there? I slowly make my way down the hill, fighting off Constables as I go.

There is no possibility of this base surviving the attack. Looking around, the forces are outnumbered three to one. Not to mention the fact our soldiers are not nearly as well trained as Constables. There is no way any of us are making it out of this battle alive.

I slash my way through Constables, dodging staffs and hydro-guns. Even at their high speeds, there is some warning. They make a slight clicking noise before they go off. If you're fast enough they can easily be avoided.

Looking at the forces we have left, the rebels aren't going to last much longer if those reinforcements don't get here soon.

I hear a loud hum, like the sound of a horn. I glance up. Over the hill is the front line of reinforcements, completely equipped with H.P.V.s. It looks like the rebels really do have a few things tucked away for crises such as these.

The new force quickly levels the playing field as I go to find their Commander. I find him at the top of the hill, watching over the battle.

He turns to me as I walk up, "Ah the infamous Nova Stargazer."

"I have to wonder how I became infamous. Am I really that memorable, or do I cause enough trouble that I'm a Constable's worst nightmare?" I sigh.

"I would place bets on you being their worst nightmare. Where is Messier?" the Commander asks.

"He was killed during the battle. However, he appointed me as the new leader. Could I get your name?" I ask walking closer.

"Seginus Nekkar, sir," he answers, straightening up and standing at attention. His lean figure tense and ready join his troops in the fight.

I wave him off. "There is no need for formalities. I had enough of that while I was a Constable. I don't need any more reminders of that time."

He nods, looking back to the battle that is slowly drawing to a close. "We will have to move this base. It is not safe now that the Council knows its location. They must have started searching the mountains."

"I agree. We will make our way to secondary, which will become the primary. Normal planning will resume there," I say, turning away from the battle to look at him. "I hope you are alright with that. I assume we wouldn't be intruding on your operations.

"It would be an honor to have you lead our base and the rebel force. However, I do not understand why we still fight. The last free hybrid was killed. We have no reason to fight now," Seginus sighs.

"I'm placing you as second in command for now. For that reason, you must know this, but you may not tell anyone. She lives. We faked her death to throw off the Council. So far it has worked, we think at least," I tell him softly, not wanting my voice to carry down to the battlefield. "There is also one other, she fights down there today, she is a bit reckless but she works very hard for the cause."

"Then we will escort the remainder of this base's occupants and supplies to ours. We have room to hold what will be left of the people," he offers, looking back to me.

"That will be fine. However, I plan to take a few Constables prisoner. I want to know how they figured out the location of this base and how long they have known we were here. We will also have to send word to our operatives in the field that home base has been compromised and moved. I will have my men erase any information we have here so the Council will have no intel. If they don't have it already. I have a feeling we may have a mole," he nods understanding me and I turn to leave.

"Oh, sir?" Seginus asks, stopping me.

I turn back around to him. "Yes?"

"I have a feeling it will be a pleasure working with you. Good luck out there," he nods to me.

"Thank you Seginus, I wish you good luck too. We are going to need all the luck we can get these next few moons," I reply, turning away once again.

I make my way back across the field of dead rebels and Constables, returning up the hill. I stop and face the small mass of rebels who survived the battle. They gather at the foot of the hill.

I speak. "We must pack up and move out now. We are no longer safe here. The reinforcements will escort us to a new base where we will set operations back up. We cannot leave a trace of information. The Council and Zubenelgenubi don't need any of our intel. We want to keep them in the dark about what we know and what we don't know. Therefore, all information is either erased or leaves with us, understand?"

The people nod in understanding and make their way back to their homes to gather up what was left of their lives.

I turn to go back into the base but find Ara standing in the doorway, staring at the battlefield. I walk past her. "That is what real war looks like. Nothing but death and destruction no matter where you look."

She races to catch up with me as I go back to the control room, "Why are you so silent? Where is Messier? Where is Pandra? Do you know if she survived?"

"Messier is dead. I have no idea about Pandra," I answer shortly.

"Who is in command then?" she asks, almost sounding

genuinely worried.

"I am."

She stares at me for a moment. "Are you sure that's a good idea, with the Council after you and everything? It will put an even larger target on your back. What's to keep them from attacking again? Who says they won't kill you? The rebels won't have a leader. Who steps up that knows what they are doing so we don't all end up dead?"

"The exact reason why Messier put me in charge. I'm the one who won't get everyone killed. I will be sure we make it through this war alive, Ara. To answer your other questions, we are moving the base and taking action before any of that can happen. We will already be enacting some of the plans that had been previously made for several attacks on the Council. They won't have another chance to attack because they won't know where we are. Besides, they will be too distracted dealing with other things to try and attack us again. Zubenelgenubi isn't going to know what hit him." I continue walking without looking back, hoping she wouldn't bring up what happened earlier.

"When were you going to come down and get me?" she asks now.

"I was heading that way when I walked in, but you were already up here so I didn't see the need to make another trip down there," I shrug.

We walk in silence for a few moments.

"Nova we need to talk. I don't mean like we are now. I mean about what happened," she sighs, sounding like she forced herself to say it.

I put my hand up, silencing her. "There is nothing to say, now forget it ever happened."

"Nova I…"

I cut her off, "I have more important things to worry about right now. If you want to live through the next few moons, shut up and let me do my job."

She comes to a halt as I keep walking, obviously giving up on trying to confront me right now. I should never have said anything, but at the moment I have to worry about the survival of what remains of this base.

I make it to the control room and gather up all the information and anything important that I can find. I grab the last two memory cards and leave, stuffing them in a bag I found. The Council can't find out anything about the rebels and our plans. It would ruin everything and endanger many.

As I make my way out of the building I see Ara with her things, helping Pandra get the rest of her stuff. I'm glad that she got the hint to pack up what little she has.

I meet back up with Commander Seginus.

"What information was left in the control room has been retrieved," I tell him.

He nods, "Then we will start evacuation immediately. The sick and the wounded will be flown to the base in the H.P.V.s, however, the rest will have to walk on foot. We do not have enough vehicles to transport everyone. We will have teams set up to escort the evacuees through the mountains."

"That should be fine. Most of us are in relatively decent condition, we should be able to make it," I say, looking out at the field as the wounded are loaded.

"The journey is about a day by H.P.V. and three days by foot. They won't be able to travel quite as fast with so many sick and wounded. However, we will send back the empty H.P.V.s to shuttle who they can after the first round of evacuees have been dropped off," Seginus explains. "Those were the emergency instructions Messier gave us in case something were to happen to a base."

"If it's what Messier wanted then we follow them, he was an excellent leader. I trust his instructions. I am going to round up the first group to take through the mountains. I will take a few of your men with me if you can spare them," I say.

"Take as many as you need. Be careful through the mountains, they can be treacherous," he warns.

"I know," I nod as I walk off, my mind going back to the mission Ara and I went on a few moons ago.

The mission to the Constable base...

That may explain how they found out our location. One of the prisoners may have been a spy, placed within the group to report back while they were confined, but decided to come with us to gather information. They wanted to know the locations of our bases. This also means we will be leading them right to the next base.

We must screen all of them when we get there and cut off all links of communication so they cannot report back. We will keep something like this from happening ever again. How could I have not seen this coming? This was a common tactic I used to gather information.

I sigh. I must have been out of it for too long. This war needs to end soon or we will end up losing it because of my silly mistakes.

I look out at the mass of rebels. They all trust me to keep them safe. How am I supposed to protect all these people when I can barely protect Ara? Maybe she was right. Maybe I am too distracted and not cut out to lead the rebels.

I shake these thoughts out of my head, no. Messier chose me. He wanted me to carry on his legacy. He wanted me to protect his people and make sure they live through this war, no matter what. He gave his life to protect them. He would expect me to be willing to do the same thing. I will, I will protect them and Ara even if it costs me my life.

Chapter Twenty-three

In the Council Dwellings

"Brother, I have news," Zubeneschamali exclaims bursting into his brother's throne room.

The hall was decorated darkly, with deep reds and blacks. Little light streamed in from the windows so the one source of light was the figure sitting comfortably in his chair picking mindlessly at the globe of his staff. He sits sideways, leaning against the armrest with his legs dangling over the opposite armrest of the throne.

"What is it?" Zubenelgenubi sighs, looking to his brother.

"The spy has reported back after the battle," Zubeneschamali says quickly.

Zubenelgenubi suddenly looked interested. "What exactly are they doing?"

"The rebels plan to move the base. Our spy has also confirmed the hybrid still lives. However, the good news is always followed by something bad. Lieutenant Stargazer has taken command of the rebels," Zubeneschamali explains.

His brother frowns deeply. "That's no good. Why hasn't General Vanil done something about his rogue Constable yet?"

"They haven't been able to catch him. They were unable to retrieve him during the battle." Zubeneschamali frowns also.

"What of the hybrid? Does she still roam free?" his brother growls, clearly upset by this turn of events.

"She does," Zubeneschamali says, fearful of what his brother is about to do.

"I want him to be put in his place as a Constable. I want her found and brought in," he exclaims. "First they escape base four fifty-two, and now this. Why can't our blasted Constables do their damn job. It's not that hard."

"I know brother, but they have proved to be..." he trails off, "more difficult than expected. General Vanil will take care of Lieutenant Stargazer. As for the hybrid, I am sure the Constables will be able to handle her." Zubeneschamali tries to soothe his brother.

"Did you not hear about what she did to the Constables at base four fifty-two? What did just I say? She killed twelve of them single-handedly and with several broken ribs. That was moons ago. Think of what she could do now. She has had time to train and hone her skills, with Stargazer's help, she is going to be more of a problem than we thought she would be. She has to be captured. She cannot be free," Zubenelgenubi exclaims.

"I did hear about that, but the Constables stationed there were fresh out of training. She may have found a batch of them that were not as advanced as the others. It could have been a simple stroke of luck." His brother searches for possible answers.

"That was no simple stroke of luck and you know it, brother. There is one thing that could explain a feat such as that. Lieutenant Stargazer trained her. We all know the trainees that were under him are the best in our force." Zubenelgenubi stands and starts to pace, his cloak swishing behind him. "You said he is Commander of the rebels now?"

His brother nods. "That is what our intel says. Messier died after being taken down by a hydro gun. I was told he specifically chose Stargazer to take over after his death. Messier was smart. He knows what Stargazer can do. I hate to say it but with Stargazer in command the rebels may be able to take us down."

"We know they have spies within the Council. We must root them out. They have meetings, to trade the information they have acquired. We will pay them twice as much to work for us and set up a trap at their next meeting for Stargazer and end his reign as the leader of the rebels. With him on our side, the war has been won for us. They will have lost their most valuable asset and we will have gained all the information we could ever need on the rebels and how they operate," Zubenelgenubi rattles off. Suddenly he stops pacing. "What about the hybrid?"

"We will bring her in too. I assume, if he trained her, they would be close. It is likely she may also become a high ranking officer within the rebels," his brother steps up. "We will have both of them and force the rest of the rebel army to surrender to the Council. They will have no reason to fight, no leader, they will have nothing."

"Is it possible..." Zubenelgenubi trails off, thinking. "We could easily make an example out of them for anyone who tries to rebel in the future."

"Brother, we must also think about what to do with these humans," Zubeneschamali suddenly brings up. "They have been key players in the rebel's plan. Most of their force is made up of the vast majority of the humans on the planet. We know the humans are smart, some are smarter than Messier was."

"They invaded our planet and tainted our race. What do you think we should do with them?" his brother asks sarcastically. "I say we should send them back to where they came from. They are beginning to take over our planet anyway. There are too many of them. If we let this continue, Ode will be overrun with humans and we will be in the minority. What happens then? We will lose control of our government and everything we hold dear. I will not allow that to happen."

"It's not that easy. Their planet no longer exists. They would have nowhere to go," Zubeneschamali argues.

"I don't care. I want them off of Ode," Zubenelgenubi exclaims.

"As you wish brother," Zubeneschamali sighs. "Also, General Vanil would like to finalize the plans to use the trigger on Lieutenant Stargazer."

His brother nods and leaves the room, wanting to have Ode under his control again.

Chapter Twenty-four

Ara

Another journey on foot, wonderful. I groan shifting my weight from side to side. Between the weight of myself and the supplies I am carrying, I feel like I have the weight of the world on my shoulders.

"Come on, we are going to have to move faster if we are ever going to make it to the new base," Nova exclaims from the front of the group.

It's been two days of walking so far. Nova said it would be about a three-day journey. As far as I know, though, every other group has already made it to the base. Nova insisted all the other groups take the H.P.V.s back so everyone would be safe quicker. We are the last group still walking, and it feels like it's going to kill me.

I reach back and pull the hood of my cloak up and over my head. The wind whips behind me, as if trying to push me along. It blows up dust around us. I greatly fear another dust storm blowing through after the one Nova and I were in.

"I can't help but notice the awkwardness between you and Nova," Pandra nudges me as we walk.

I glance at Nova, who walks at the head of the group. "He hasn't said a word to me this entire journey. His sole focus has been getting these people to the new base safely. He could have easily said something though, something short and quick. He could have told me he wanted to talk once we arrived, but nothing, not a word, not even a glance in my direction to see if I'm alright."

Pandra frowns. "Don't ask me, I don't know the reasoning behind anything he does. I bet you have a better idea. Ara, you can't let this keep happening to the two of you. The rebels can't have their best two agents constantly at odds. You had to have done something to get him to ignore

145

you like this."

I draw my staff and lean on it as I walk, hoping to catch his attention. Nothing. Not even acting hurt can get him to shift his gaze onto me.

"I didn't think I did anything to upset him. Yes, I didn't stay where he told me to, but he didn't really expect me to follow that command in the first place did he? He should have known I wasn't going to sit and wait to be killed," I sigh.

Pandra shakes her head, disappointed.

Gosh, it seems like no matter what we do one of us is always being cold to the other. We can never catch a break, can we?

Suddenly, a low hum snaps me from my thoughts. I see several H.P.V.s heading in our direction. Maybe we won't have to walk the rest of this journey on foot.

"I don't think I have ever been happier to see an H.P.V. If we walk much farther I think my feet may fall off." Pandra laughs, trying to lighten up my sour mood.

I glower at her, now is not the time to laugh and make jokes. The H.P.V.s land and we load them quickly. Everyone wants to get to the base so they can rest.

As we lift off my thoughts start to wander again. I would like to think Nova has my best interests in mind but sometimes I have to think otherwise. I don't believe becoming the leader of the rebels is the best idea right now, especially with him being the Council's number one threat and the most wanted Oderian on the planet. I fear he is going to get himself killed over something meaningless because he thinks he has to defend it.

As I sit there I find myself growing more and more cross with him. He didn't even ask me if it was alright with me for him to become the leader of this whole operation. Why should he have to ask me though? It's not like my life could be in danger or anything.

I sigh. Distancing myself may be my best option. I need to get away from him and all this insanity.

No. He is the one that is distancing himself. He is the one

who has not talked to me for days. If he doesn't want to look at me, then so be it. I will make the best of my alone time.

I storm off the H.P.V. when it lands. I don't look back to see if Pandra follows me. I glance at a map of the base quickly then head to the training center. I need to kill something.

A while later I find myself beating up a bag full a dirt with my staff, imagining it was a Constable, especially the one from the mission.

"You. Stupid. Piece. Of. Crap," I huff at the bag, suddenly imagining that it was Nova. "You. Try. To. Make. Things. Up. With. Me. But. You. Still. Ignore. Me." I slam my staff into it and send it flying across the floor.

I stare at it, my chest heaving. I drop my staff, suddenly aware of what I had been thinking and doing. I had beaten the crap out of Nova inside my head. I must be going insane. This war is driving me to insanity. It must be.

I scream in frustration and pick up my staff, hurling it at the bag. It splits open, and spills the dirt on the floor of the training room. I walk over to it, my feet scuffing in the dirt. I scoop up my staff and brush it off then slide it back into the holster slung across my back.

This war has ruined my entire life. I'm not the same Oderian I was moons ago. Hell, I'm not even an Oderian or a human, I'm some weird mixture of the two. At least Nova still has everything going for him.

Maybe I should try to talk to him, maybe I could get him to explain what is going on and actually have a conversation about what he said the other day without him putting me off about it.

I leave the training room and make my way to the control room knowing someone would clean up the mess I made at some point. At the moment, I have more pressing matters to worry about.

I press the button, opening the door and see him standing there at the head of the table. Discussing battle plans, of course. I lean against the wall, wondering if anyone even noticed my presence.

"After the last attack, I did some very serious thinking. How could the Council have found out the location of our base? We have a mole. I believe they came from the rescue mission a few moons ago. It is a common tactic to place an agent undercover in prisons. It gives Constables someone to get information through without having to press the prisoners for it. I think one came along, thinking they would relay what information they could get back to the Council," Nova says.

"What's to keep them from revealing the location of this base?" a human seated at the table asks.

"I have everyone rescued on the mission secured. They believe everyone is quarantined for security purposes. They have no communication with each other or the outside world, and it must stay that way. They cannot know we have figured out there was a mole. This would ruin our plans. At my next meeting with our Council spies, I will set them on a course to find out who that mole is through their sources. They will have an easier time finding out than we will," Nova explains. He glances around the table. "That is all, you may go."

Once everyone has left, I slowly make my way up to Nova, "Thanks for greeting me as I came in," I say sarcastically.

"I saw you. I wouldn't have let you stay in here if you were someone else," he says, not even looking up at me.

"That makes me feel so much better," I roll my eyes, "We need to talk."

He shakes his head, still looking down at the hologram table. "Not right now, Ara. I don't have time."

"No Nova," I say harshly. "You are not going to shove me away for a second time."

He finally looks up at me. "Later."

I groan setting my hands down on the table. "It's always something with you isn't it? Oh, I was a Constable, oh, I'm trying to keep you safe, oh, I'm busy trying to lead the rebels."

He glares at me. "Leave, Ara."

I shake my head. "Not happening until you decide to actually talk to me and not ignore me."

"You are testing my patience," he growls.

"Yes, I am, because I am sick of being overlooked. You can't tell someone you love them then ignore them for days. There is nothing okay with that. So, I'm going to test your small amount of patience until you break and talk to me," I exclaim, finally letting out all my anger.

He sighs and sinks down into a chair. "I really don't have time for this. We have a war to fight."

"So, a war is more important than me? Thanks for caring so much Nova," I hiss and leave, not wanting to deal with him anymore.

I can practically feel my hearts dropping lower and lower as I walk away from the Control room. What he is doing to me really isn't right. One moment he says he loves me, the next the rebels are more important.

There for one bright moment I thought we could win this war and everything I imagined would come true. Obviously, thinking that was a mistake. How could I ever think I would be that important to a person? So important they would do anything for me.

I wish I knew his motives, part of me says he has a reason for being so cold. Another part of me says his coldness is because the war is bringing that side out of him.

I fear what else it may bring out of him. I never want to see the true Constable side of him. A war really does bring out the worst in people. Hate and betrayal mostly.

I finally find my way to my new room and sit down on the edge of the regeneration tube, maybe I need rest. Maybe everything will be okay then.

After a long rest in the regeneration tube, I decide to get up and polish my staff. I run the cloth along it and around the globe, suddenly transfixed by its swirls and deep colors.

"Ara?" a soft voice calls.

I glance up and see Nova standing guiltily in the doorway. "What do you want?" I ask harshly.

"To talk," he answers.

"Hmm, I think I should turn you away because I'm too busy to talk to you. Maybe then you will see how I feel." I look back down at my staff.

"Ara," Nova sighs, stepping into the room. "I'm sorry. I have been so busy these last few days with the rebels, the mole, the battle and the move of the bases..." he trails off.

"That gives you no excuse for pushing me away," I shake my head.

"I know, I know and I'm sorry. I have been trying to protect you," he sighs, looking to the floor.

"Now that we are back on better terms than we were a few moons ago I think your job of protecting me sucks and you need to try a different method," I huff.

He nods. "Then what do you want me to do?"

"I want you to act like a friend. With everything that is going on right now, we need friends to confide in. This war is starting to get to all of us and pushing each other away is not going to help." I look back up to him. "I don't care that you are leading the rebels now but you need to pay attention to the things you don't want to lose."

I pick up my staff and leave the room to let him contemplate what had happened, maybe he will see his wrong doing and fix it, or maybe he won't.

The base seems quiet as I walk, usually it is filled with movement and talking but I see no one as I make my way to the doors at the front of the base. I push one open and walk outside into the cool, dark night air. I sigh in disappointment when my glow doesn't flicker on. It never has, so why should I expect it to now.

I sink into the dust and lean against the wall of the base, pulling my cloak tightly around myself. Staring up at the stars, I draw the constellations with my eyes. The stars shine down brightly as if there is nothing wrong in the world, like there is no war or pain or death, only their silvery star light.

My mind once again wanders back to a simpler time when Nova and I would lay out and look at the stars all night. Somehow, he had a comprehensive knowledge of them and taught me everything I know. I close my eyes imagining that one night...

~ * ~

He points up to another cluster of stars, "That is Ara."

"Like my name?" I ask, "Why was I named after a bunch of stars?"

150

"When the humans came here they brought their constellations. You were named after one of them. The constellation is the altar on which the Greek gods swore unity against the Titans, their evil predecessors, who they eventually overthrew and became rulers of the Earth," Nova explains.

"That's an interesting story," I sigh, still staring up at my constellation. *"They really look beautiful tonight."*

Nova nods, *"Yes, they do."*

I shiver and wrap my cloak closer around me, not having a glow to keep myself warm. Nova notices this and pulls me closer, engulfing me in his glow, quickly warming me up. "Is that better?" he asks in a whisper.

"Much," I answer.

~ * ~

We stared at the stars all night that night. It soon became a nightly ritual. He would teach me and we would stare at the sky for hours.

I blink back tears at the memory, sadly that's all it is. There will never be a time like that again. I fear this war is going to destroy everything I have ever known and possibly even my future.

I jump when I hear someone sit down next to me. I look over not surprised to see Nova beside me.

"I thought I would find you out here." He glances up at the sky. "Were you remembering the first night we stared at the stars?"

I give a slight nod, looking back up.

"Ara, I am going to be honest with you..." Nova says softly. "I think we are going to die trying to win this war. The Council has so much more than we do. I think we are in way over our heads."

"I agree," I say in a whisper. "Where else are we going to go? There is nowhere to hide from the Council unless it's with the rebels. Even now it's a matter of time before they find us again, and they will. I have no doubt in my mind they will find us. They will kill every single person who even thought about rebelling against them, no matter if they are human or Oderian. Besides, right now I would rather die fighting for my life than be executed because I'm a little different from everyone else. If the Council wants to be like that then I want to go down with a bang. They are going to remember me."

Nova sighs. "It was a mistake coming here. We should have stayed in the mountains. With a mole, the Council will soon find out you aren't really dead and come after us with a full force. I don't want that to happen. I didn't want any of this to happen."

"The one thing we can do now is fight to the best of our abilities. The Council will most likely beat us, but I think we should make it hard for them. We will not go down without a fight. Even if I have to kill Constables one by one myself, they are going to have a hard time taking me out." I glance over at Nova as he nods in approval.

"I'll be right there with you," he sighs.

"I do have fears, though," I mumble to him.

"Like what?" he asks.

"I fear failing everyone here. They rely on the two of us so much if I make one wrong move, everyone is dead and it's going to be my fault," I whisper.

Nova sighs. "There is always a chance of failure. No matter what you do. There is a chance that everyone is going to die, but it will have been their choice. They chose to fight after all. You can't put more blood on your hands then you can handle, there is no point. There will come a time, when you can't count the number of people you have killed but you have to put it in the back of your mind. If you don't you will never escape their faces. Every time I close my eyes, I can see them. Don't become what I have Ara."

"I'm not going to." I shake my head. I glance back up at the stars, then around at our dark world. "Nova." I turn back to him. "Let's go back inside."

I stand and he follows me back in. "What are your plans to end this?"

"Spies, mainly. They are all the inside information we have. I plan to meet with them in a moon, then the rest of our plans will be able to continue," he says as we walk.

"We can't win this war without actually engaging the Council. There is going to be a battle worse than this past one." I turn to look at him as we walk. His face is set into a hard grimace.

"I know, and many will not make it through that battle," he says through gritted teeth.

"I know you hate it, but a sacrifice has to be made or those who have already died will have died in vain and for what? For us to give up? No, we started this and we are going to end it..." I trail off. "Even if it costs us our lives."

Nova nods as we stop in front of the door to my room. "Get some rest; the next few moons are going to be ugly."

I nod, and head into my room, watching as Nova walks down the hall to his. Sighing, I hit the button to close the door, leaning against it once it slides shut.

I want the Nova I knew before the war back, the carefree Nova. The one who isn't constantly haunted by the faces and voices of his victims. It is clear to me he is trying to keep it together but sometimes his anger gets the best of him. The Council has turned him into something I can't fix, something no one can.

I lie down in my regeneration tube and quickly fall into a dream state.

~ * ~

"Nova?" I call out as I walk down the hall of the base. "Where are you?"

He suddenly appears around the corner holding his staff.

"Nova, we need to talk about what has happened. I don't mean like we did earlier, we need to actually sit down and discuss what you said," I say as I walk up to him.

"No, I need to talk to you," he grunts turning to me.

"About what?" I ask, he doesn't look all that happy to see me.

"We have made a deal with the Council that will end the war," he says, looking down at me emotionlessly.

"Alright. What do you have to do?" His expression scares me.

"They said that they will let the rest of the rebels live if..." he pauses.

"If what?" I urge him on.

"If I kill you," he breathes.

"What? And you agreed to this deal?" I exclaim, backing away from him.

"You said that you wanted to win this war even if you had to sacrifice yourself," he shrugs, taking a step forward for every step I take back.

"No, I didn't mean it like that," I try to explain quickly.

"That's what I thought you meant. So, would you like to die here privately or make it a spectacle for the whole rebel force to enjoy?" he asks, a smirk playing on his lips.

"Neither," I yelp and push past him, running down the hall.

"You won't be able to run from me forever Ara," he laughs as he chases after me.

"I can sure try," I scream back as I make it to the doors of the base. I burst through them and skid to a stop when I see the entire army of rebels below me.

"Please Ara," Nova says as he grabs me from behind, "Don't make this any harder than it has to be. It's the only way."

"No," I gasp as I struggle in his vice like grip. "We could keep fighting and not give into the Council like this. This is exactly what they wanted. Let me go."

"Sorry," Nova whispers as I feel a searing pain in my side.

I glance down, my throat constricting at the sight of the blood. So much blood. Nova lets go of me and I fall to my knees.

"Nova w-why?" I manage to choke.

~ * ~

I jump out of my dream state hearing someone screaming. I quickly realize it was me who was screaming. My chest heaves as I whip my head around looking at the room.

Suddenly the lights flicker on and the door opens, allowing Nova to step into the room holding his staff. "Is everything alright?" he exclaims.

"S-stay away from me," I gasp, remnants of the dream flashing before my eyes. "Please don't kill me." I hold my arms up as if to protect myself, still slightly disorientated from the dream.

"Ara." Nova grabs my arms and brings them down. "Ara it's okay. You were in your dream state that's all. You are perfectly safe right here."

I try to shove his hands away. "Let go of me."

He immediately removes his hands, stepping away from me, a look of sadness clouding his face.

"The dream was about me wasn't it?" he asks.

I nod, starting to catch my breath. "It was."

"I was trying to kill you," he mumbles.

"You did kill me," I say, sitting up and holding my head in my hands.

"I didn't realize I had scared you that much. I'm sorry, I-I should leave. You shouldn't want me around after that," Nova whispers as he starts to back out of the room.

I shake my head, "No, please stay. I need the company. I'm not going to be able to get any more rest after that."

He hesitantly steps back into the room, "Are you sure?"

"I am. Besides, dreams are harmless," I shrug.

"Our subconscious shows us things we don't see in the real world through dreams," Nova says as he sits down next to me.

"I don't care what my subconscious knows, if I don't realize it consciously then it's not worth knowing." I stare at the wall, trying to clear my head.

"I wouldn't say that about all things. Sometimes you have to listen to yourself, if you do, it's usually right," Nova says barely above a whisper.

"Well, I'm not always right, so I don't listen to myself. I listen to the world around me then figure it out from there," I contradict him.

"That's one way to do it," Nova cracks a half smile.

"I don't think the Council members have a subconscious or listen to the world around them because whatever is telling them to do what they are doing is wrong very, very wrong." I glance at Nova, who stares at the wall like I did.

"I agree. They need to start listening to the people of Ode and see their mistakes," he sighs.

We sit there in silence for a while, enjoying each other's company as best we could while trying to put everything that happened behind us.

"I'm sorry for what I have done to give you dreams like that. You already have enough to deal with thanks to the Council deciding they hate you," Nova whispers.

"It's alright. This war is more than enough to give me dreams like that, it's impossible to escape them. Do you have them too?" I ask.

Nova barely nods, "I have dreams that I'm killing innocent people like I did when I was a Constable."

"Tell me about them, I have nothing better to do anyway." I look at him expectantly.

"There is one that haunts me the most. Let me say this first, however, I had no choice. I begged and pleaded for them not to make me do this but they forced me to. I had moved up in the ranks by this time. The Council had been receiving threats from an Oderian and so we were sent out to find him and kill him...and his family to stop him from enacting anything." Nova stops for a moment.

I can tell this is really hard for him.

"H-he had a wife and children. The other Constables, they were relentless. They made the two kids watch as they killed their parents. Then they made me kill them."

Nova drops his head in his hands. I set my hand on his back, trying to calm him some.

"I didn't want to do it. I really didn't. Their looks of horror and pain don't go away. Every time I close my eyes, I see them, those two kids. A-and I know what they were thinking, they were thinking I was a monster with no mercy to kill both of them. I had no choice, though..." he trails off.

"I remember hearing about that," I whisper.

"I'm sorry. I did many things as a Constable that I regret, and I can't take any of it back. I'm going to have to live with those things for the rest of my life," he shakes his head, as if trying to wipe the memories from his head. "So every night, I dream about those two children's lives I stole, I dream about the life they could have had if I had not given into the pressure and stood up for them. I may have died in the process but I would have died with a clear conscience."

"Nova, there is no point in blaming yourself for what happened. It wasn't really you that killed them. It was the Council and now, you are standing up for them by resisting the Council and leading the rebellion against them. You will avenge their wrongful deaths. You will avenge many wrongful deaths." I try to bring his spirits up a bit.

He seems to put it all behind him for the moment and stands up. "You better get ready, we will be leaving to talk to the spies soon."

With that, he leaves the room without another word. Classic Nova, upset about something one moment, the next he is cold as stone.

I groan, stretching as I stand. I guess I do have to get ready. The suns are starting to rise. Carefully, I take my staff down off the wall, where I had hung it before resting.

Moments later the team is loaded into the H.P.V. and sitting silently. Every time we go on a mission like this it seems like no one has anything to say because they are all too afraid of dying.

We land a way away from a Constable base and sneak in silently. Nova said this would be the last meeting with the spies so there is no point in leaving any surviving Constables. Besides the more we take out now, the less we will have to take out later on.

Chapter Twenty-five

Ara

I let out a groan as another Constable goes limp, falling on top of me. I shove him off and look to Nova as he laughs slightly.

"Oh yes Ara, meeting our spies in a place where there are tons of Constables is a great idea. They would never suspect us of doing such a thing," I mumble to myself mimicking Nova as we walk.

I think I've killed six Constables already. However, Nova has me beat with ten lying dead in his wake.

One walks around the corner and without even thinking I hurl my staff at him. He falls to the ground dead. I yank it out of his lifeless body as we walk by.

"That's seven, Nova. You better step up, I'm gaining on you," I smirk as I turn to face him, walking backward along the hallway.

"We're almost there, don't worry. Besides there will be more on the way out." He rolls his eyes at me.

Moments later, we stop at a closed door. He motions for me to stand behind him as he punches the button to open the door. It slides open silently and Nova steps into the room.

Two Oderians sit at a table, facing the door. They stand as Nova and I walk in. One nods to Nova as they sit down. I stick my staff in its holster and stand guard at the door. I have no place sitting at that table with them.

They talk too quietly for me hear, the less people who know the information the easier it will be to keep it a secret, whatever it is.

Nova glances up at me then back to the two spies, and they continue to whisper. I have a feeling the main topic of this conversation is me. I stand there awkwardly, trying to ignore the whisper of my name every once in a while.

They talk for quite a while. Suddenly I hear an alarm blaring. I look to Nova and say, "We need to leave, now."

He nods and stands up, thanking the two spies and telling them to continue to gather what information they can get on the Council and whoever is leading it.

We make our way out of the room and down the hall, glancing over our shoulders every few moments to make sure we aren't being followed.

"There they are." I hear a Constable yell from behind us.

I glance back and see a swarm of Constables. "Run," I exclaim.

Nova and I race out of the building and to the H.P.V. that waits for us. We jump on and Nova yells to the pilot, "Let's go now." The rest of the team sits, prepared to fight if necessary.

The H.P.V. rumbles and takes off as the Constables come running out of the building.

"That was close," I sigh in relief once we are a safe distance away from the base. I glance at Nova who sits in silence.

"What did they say?" I ask.

He shakes his head, "Things I am not allowed to inform you of."

I roll my eyes. "Come on Nova. You know you can trust me. It's not like I'm going to go off and tell everyone what happened. Besides, I heard my name and Pandra's several times."

"You must have been mistaken, and once again I can't tell you," he says sternly.

I shrug. "Okay, then."

We sit in silence for the rest of the flight.

I have to wonder what he is keeping from me. I look over and he seems to be lost in thought, not even noticing my gaze. I sigh, whatever it is, it can't be good. He is quiet like that when he is thinking very hard about something. This worries me, whatever he is planning has something to do with me.

We land back at base and I head to my room to put away my staff.

Nova goes off in another direction, his face looking rather pale, still lost in thought about whatever he and the spies discussed.

He doesn't look too happy to tell the other rebel leaders what the spies told him.

I open the door to my room as I press my lips in a thin line. I know it's something that has to do with me. That is the one reason why he wouldn't tell me what was said.

I hang up my staff carefully, thinking I could go and listen in on his conversation with the other rebel leaders.

I silently make my way to the control center. I hear a voice ask, "What did they say? Was it good news?"

I think that's Seginus, Nova's second in command.

"It wasn't good. None of it was what I wanted to hear. Our plans are going to have to change," Nova sighs.

"Explain," Seginus urges him on.

"The twins are at it again. Plotting and scheming. They plan to use the trigger then go after her." I hear Nova's footsteps as he paces.

What is the trigger? What's so scary about it?

"You know there is nothing I can do if they use the trigger. I will be rendered useless to everyone but them," Nova exclaims.

"I know," Seginus huffs, clearly frustrated.

"They plan to attack again soon, take Ara and me in and use us as examples if anyone else tries to rebel. We can't lose this base. They have won if this base falls. We have too many innocents here that will die if the Council takes us over," Nova continues.

"We must act quickly then. Our plans need to be put into action as soon as possible," Seginus says quickly.

What plans do they have? Suddenly I hear footsteps come toward the door. I jump away and race down the hall, hopeful they didn't hear or see me.

There are still so many things he doesn't tell me. Who knows what he could be keeping from me. I need to know what his plans are. How am I supposed to know what to do if this base gets attacked? What if the Council uses that trigger thing on Nova?

I jump when an alarm starts to go off. I hear yelling and troops race down the halls. I run to my room and grab my staff from where it hung. It will be my luck that we get attacked again. I can never catch a break, can I?

I weave through the troops making my way out of the building. I gasp, looking around at the battle field. Bodies lay scattered everywhere. Constables quickly make their way toward the base.

How did they find us again? We left no trace. I stumble back as I realize something. They must have followed us back to the base after the mission earlier today. It's our fault they are here.

I whip around and run back into the building yelling, "Nova, Nova." My arms pump at my sides as I slide around corners.

I skid to a stop in front of the control room door as the alarms continue to blare. "Nova, Nova." I hit the button to open the door several times but the door refuses to slide out of the way. "Nova, Seginus, open the door, now."

I continue to bang on it until I hear the click and the hiss of the door opening. Nova stands on the other side of it confused and glaring at me. "What's happening? Why are the alarms going off?"

"The Constables followed us here. They are going to take this base too if we don't do something," I gasp, trying to catch my breath.

His eyes go wide, and he mutters a curse under his breath then turns back to Seginus. "I want you to go prepare the troops. No Constable can survive this battle to tell others where we are hiding."

Seginus nods and quickly exits the room, leaving Nova and me alone.

"I'm going to ask you to go hide once again. You don't need to take any part in this battle," Nova says, turning back to me while preparing his staff.

I shake my head, "I'm not hiding like I did last time. Have I not proved I can fight yet? I defeated more than half a dozen when we went to the meeting with the spies. I defeated more than that with a broken rib at the Constable base. How can you not trust me yet?"

"I do trust you. I don't want to take any risks. You are the last of your known kind, and you do not need to die during one measly battle."

Nova starts to make his way out of the room and I follow him.

"I am going to fight." I stand my ground as I walk behind him.

"You need to follow orders," he chimes back at me.

I stop walking and say defiantly, "No."

"What?" He stops dead in his tracks and slowly turns towards me. "No?"

"This is not your fight Nova. It never has been. This has always been my fight and my war, no matter what you would like to think. This entire war is because I and others like me exist. So no, you are not going to stop me from fighting my fight no matter how much you claim to love me. You can't use that as an excuse this time and catch me off guard. You lied anyway. You should consider yourself lucky I'm even speaking to you right now," I spit and shove him out of the way, continuing down the hall in a fit of rage.

I am so sick of him being ignorant. If he is upset with me then he can suck it up because I am going to fight no matter what. He is the one keeping me in the dark. I have told him everything he needs to know.

I find myself at the door of the base once again. I push it open, taking in the sight for a second time, this time more bodies lay scattered at the base of the hill. The air is thick with the smell of blood, and the ground is stained with its purple color.

I race down the hill before Nova can come out of the building and try to stop me again. I yank my staff out of its holster and slam the end into the head of a Constable that has his back to me.

"You should have been watching your back," I sneer as he falls to the ground with a thump.

I hear the click of a hydro gun and duck quickly as it shoots over my head. I jump up, breaking the globe at the top of my staff and shoving it into the Constable's soft torso.

I pull it free, puffing a wisp of hair out of my face. I hear a Constable coming up behind me and I spin around, slashing at his neck. He quickly joins the other Constables on the ground.

I glance around and see Seginus fending off a group of them. I fight my way over to him, letting out my anger on the enemies. Constables are dropping to the ground with every step I take.

Once I make it to him, we fight side by side, the mound of Constables growing with each slash of our staffs.

"You fight a lot like Nova," Seginus says as he stands catching his breath, waiting for another Constable daring enough to approach us.

"He's the one who trained me," I growl through gritted teeth, pushing a few bodies away to give me a little more room to move.

Seginus grunts in response as he notices a slash on his upper leg. He kneels down to tend to it as I keep watch. I turn away scanning the field and watch as the last few Constables begin to fall.

"Ara," a strangled cry reaches my ears and I whip around to see a Constable trying to hold down a struggling Seginus.

With a blink of an eye, my staff thuds into the upper chest of the Constable and he falls backward off of Seginus. I race over to him, "Are you alright?"

He nods as he shakily pushes himself up. "I'm fine. I couldn't grab my staff, he disarmed me and had me pinned before I could do anything."

He picks up his staff which had been tossed out of reach and glances around.

I look around for the first time since the Constables decided to leave us alone. I realize the reason they stopped coming at us was because there were no more. At a glance all I see are our troops standing alone or in pairs with Constables lying around them.

The rest of our enemies must have retreated due to the significant loss in their numbers. I let out a sigh of relief. We got lucky once again that the assault was not as bad as I originally thought it to be.

Chapter Twenty-six

Nova

I stand at the top of the hill and watch as Ara comes back to the base after fighting alongside Seginus.

She brushes past me muttering, "I'll be in my room." She then disappears into the base, not even glancing back at the horrific battle field.

I don't move from my spot at the top of the hill for quite a while. By the time I snapped out of my daze everyone had already gone back into the base to regroup after the battle.

I jump at the sudden sound of an explosion. The lights surrounding the base flicker out. I look around, the outside of the base now illuminated by my glow. Slowly the light gets brighter. There is someone here with me. I immediately get tense, ready for whatever may happen.

Several Constables come from around the corner of the building.

"There he is," one exclaims.

I draw my staff pointing it at them menacingly. "What do you want?"

"We want you to show us what you did with the girl. We want to be sure she is dead and we were not tricked," one of them says as I hear footsteps behind me.

I whip around and find four more Constables approaching me. I'm out numbered. I glance at their uniforms. The deep purple tells me they are part of the specially trained force. I may have trained them and taught them everything they know. In a fight, a group of them can easily take out someone of their own skill level or greater.

Suddenly I hear another explosion from the other side of the building, but this one is bigger and louder. I stand there dazed, my ears ringing from the noise.

They seize me by my arms and pull me toward the door before I even have the chance to react. I should have seen this coming.

"Good to see you again, Nova Stargazer. You remember me?" one Constable asks.

I groan. This had been one of my trainees a long time ago. "Of course, I remember you. No one I have ever trained could be as cowardly as you."

"So where is the girl?" the Constable asks, not even fazed by the remark of his old teacher.

"Do you really think she is still alive? She's dead. Get it through your thick skulls," I laugh, wincing slightly from my still ringing ears.

The Constable snickers at my comment. "We know she is alive, but if you keep lying to us then we will make sure we blow up the building with her inside it."

"No," I exclaim. "There are innocent people in there. They don't deserve a fate such as that."

"I don't care about them," the Constable growls. "Show me where the girl is."

"Fine," I sigh. The needs of the many outweigh the needs of one.

I put my staff into its holster slung across my back and turn toward the door.

There is no point in trying to fight back, there are too many Constables here and they have an entire army to call in as backup. I can't risk the entire base's safety. I guess I have to show them where Ara is. I hope she's alright. I hope she is ready to fight for her life for the second time today.

Chapter Twenty-seven

Ara

To be honest, I really hope Nova comes and speaks to me about what I said earlier, but as the lights flicker out I begin to doubt myself, even though I hear someone's footsteps coming down the hallway through the door of my room.

I sit quietly and listen. The footsteps seem to be echoing closer and closer. It sounds as if there are five people walking down the hall. I don't think that it's Nova. He wouldn't be with that many people at once. It draws too much attention.

As I stand up, I press myself against the wall and feel for something I can use as a weapon. My staff is on the other side of the room, hanging on the wall. It would be too risky to try to make my way over there in the dark. I could trip and fall, alerting whoever is in the hall that I am here. My hands wrap around a metal pipe, quickly tearing it off, I slide along the wall until I feel the door next to me and hold up the pipe, prepared to beam whoever it is upside the head.

The footsteps sound as if they are a few paces from the door. It slides open, still, no light seeps into the room. Then my Oderian DNA suddenly decides to kick in, and I start to glow. Of all the times my glow could come back, it had to choose now. I quickly slip around to the other side of the regeneration tube to get farther away from the door.

"I see her," a man exclaims.

"Shoot," I mutter. This is not good, not good at all.

"Ara?" a muffled voice asks. I take a few steps back away from the tube, hoping that my glow will go out.

That's Nova's voice, why can't I see him glowing? Why is his voice muffled?

"Nova, is that you?" I ask, to make sure, still holding up the pipe. I shouldn't have asked if there is someone with him. I think they are looking for me.

"Run Ara, run," he exclaims.

Suddenly the lights flicker on, and my eyes widen. There are four Constables. Two hold back Nova, with a third standing slightly behind them, and the fourth seems to be their leader as he stands in front of them, looking proud of himself. Nova's face, neck, and hands are covered. I guess so I wouldn't see his glow. The Constables are also covered, except for their silver eyes, which glow evilly even in the light.

I drop the pipe and turn to run, my odds here aren't very good if I don't have an actual weapon, but before I can even take a step, I am tackled to the ground.

"Get off me," I screech as I try to shove the Constable off.

I hit him in the face as he grabs for my hands, eventually catching them and pinning my wrists to the floor.

My chest heaves from fighting back as I finally give in. I watch as the leader pulls the cover off Nova's head.

His gaze lands on me and something inside him explodes. He tears himself from the Constables and throws them against the wall.

Once again, I attempt to shove the Constable off me, but fail because he is much stronger than me. It's like I'm being squished, I can't breathe. I can't do anything Nova taught me.

"Nova, help!" I gasp.

He turns and his gaze falls on me, but before he has a chance to do anything, the previous two Constables pin him to the wall. "Let go of me," he growls as he struggles against their tight grip.

The Constable that was on top of me stands and pulls me up, holding me in place. As I squirm against the Constable, I hear a click and a hiss. Snapping my head up, I see one injecting the same stuff that almost killed me moons ago, into Nova.

They empty the tube, and he stops struggling. The Constables pull him away from the wall and shove him toward me. He stumbles and falls to the floor groaning. I know exactly what he feels like right now.

"Nova," I exclaim. "No," I cry. I can feel my throat starting to close up, and I let out a quiet sob. No matter how bad our disagreements are, he is still the one person I have left.

The Constable lets go of me and pushes me toward Nova. I take a few steps before I fall to my knees next to him.

His eyes fight to stay open as he looks at me. Then they slowly start to slide closed, the drug taking effect.

"No, no, Nova do not close your eyes, stay awake," I cry out as I gently shake his shoulders.

"Ara," he says softly. "Run, get away from here."

"I won't leave you here for the Constables," I whisper, shaking my head.

"Go. I'll be fine. I will see you soon. This is your fight after all," Nova breathes as he lightly pushes me away.

I stand up and turn away, glancing at the Constables before taking off. Running as fast as I can down the hall and up the stairs, I blink back tears. The Constables run after me, yelling for someone to stop me.

I turn and run into the room where Nova and I had been training, I quickly turn back around and slam my fist into the button to close the door. It slides shut, clicking as it locks.

Resting my back against the door I hold my head in my hands. A loud sob escapes my lips.

They kidnapped Nova. They are going to kill him or use that trigger he was talking about. What am I going to do?

Nova was holding me together, keeping me safe. He saved me. He loves me. Why do I see what I had after I have already lost it?

I stand up and suck in an unsteady breath. I am going to be strong. I am going to save him. This is my war and I am going to fight it.

Chapter Twenty-eight

Ara

A long while later, after I paced and planned the door suddenly flies open.

"Ara are you alright?" A worried Seginus asks, scaring me out of my dazed state. Glad I unlocked the door earlier, I see he has several cuts on his face and arms that hadn't been there when I left him after the battle. Behind him is Pandra who looks slightly better. The Constables must have gotten to them too. I walk up to Seginus, lightly brushing his cheek with my fingers. "Did they get to you too?" I ask.

He nods. "They wanted to know where you were. I didn't tell them. They weren't very happy with me after that."

"Well, either way, they did find me," I sigh. "What about you Pandra?"

She shakes her head, "No, this was all from the battle."

Seginus winces slightly as he shifts his weight from foot to foot awkwardly.

"Do you need someone to tend to those? There's a kit here," I ask.

"I would greatly appreciate it," Seginus nods as he slides down the wall and leans against it.

I grab the kit from where Nova and I stashed it in case anything happened while we were training. "They cut you up pretty good, didn't they?"

"Only Constables." Pandra rolls her eyes as she sits down next to me, handing me things as I hold my hand out to her.

"They did, and I'll tell you, I don't ever want to be on the other side of a staff that sharp ever again," he mumbles as I carefully clean the cuts and slashes.

"That's why we fight," I reply.

"Do you want to have a look at my leg too? Saves me a trip and some pain," he asks.

"No problem." I bend down, tearing his pant leg open a little more so I can have a closer look at the gash. "How did you even walk down here with that?" I ask. "I wouldn't have been able to stand up."

Pandra takes one look before turning away gagging.

Seginus shrugs, "I have other things on my mind right now."

I quickly clean the wound and wrap a bandage around it tightly to keep it clean and uninfected. "How did they find you? The lights were out?" Seginus asks suddenly.

"My glow came back for a few moments. That's how they found me," I sigh.

"Your glow came back?" he gasps.

"Really?" Pandra turns back, surprised. "Mine went out long ago and has never even flickered on for a few seconds since."

"It did," I nod.

"Say, do you know where Nova went? I can't find him," he asks as I help him up from the floor.

I turn away from him shaking my head and say, "Nova isn't here. The Constables have him."

His forced smile quickly turns into a deep set frown. "He can't be gone. Who will lead the rebels now? I am not equipped to lead."

"You aren't equipped to run the base?" I ask. "You are the second in command? Don't...don't you have a protocol for things like this?" The rebel force is without a leader. If there is no rebel leader, there is no mission, no mission, no Nova.

He shrugs. "I'm not great with creating battle strategies. It's a wonder I ever made my way this far up the ladder."

"Why don't you do it, Ara?" Pandra pipes in.

I glance at her, shaking my head, "I don't know..."

"Nova taught you everything you would need to know. You could do it, Ara. Without you there will be no mission to save what it left of our race, there will be nothing left for Nova to return to," Pandra urges.

"I'll offer what guidance I can," Seginus says.

"Alright, I will step up in Nova's place. We will be going on that mission to save the hybrids, and we will save Nova. If he is already dead, his death will not be in vain," I declare.

"Thank you, Ara, the rebels would be nothing without you. Now please come with me because we need to plan our attack on the council," Seginus thanks me as he turns.

Pandra pats me on the back encouragingly as we leave the training room.

I follow them out of the room and to the Control room. As we walk in, I see many people have gathered here to help come up with a plan.

I stand at the head of the table and everyone stares at me. I take a deep breath, you can do it, do it for Nova.

"Where is Nova?" one person asks the question everyone else is probably thinking.

"Nova is gone. He was taken by the Constables. We must continue planning the mission. Time is of the essence," I announce calmly.

Everyone nods. "Then let's get to work," Seginus says.

I click the button on the table, and it lights up, revealing the plans that had already been made.

"Ma'am I know we have to execute this mission, but we don't have the supplies left to do anything because of the attack this morning," one man says meekly.

Another man turns to him. "There is a Council Arsenal not far from the dwellings. If we raid that then attack, we might have a chance."

I nod. "That will work. Now, we will have two teams. One will clear the way for the other. That team will then make their way into the dwellings and rescue the hybrids, then go after the Council. Exactly as Nova planned previously for this mission."

"I concur. Two teams would be the most effective," a man agrees.

For quite a while longer we plan the attack and come up with several backup plans in case something goes wrong.

My head rests in my hands. I let out a sigh as they continue to debate about different things.

I jump to my feet and throw my hands in the air, "I'm sick of this. I need some time alone." Seginus looks at me sadly but nods, telling me that I am free to leave if I wish to.

Everyone stares as I storm out of the room. Quickly racing down the halls, I reach the training center in a matter of seconds.

My feet guide me to the wall of staves, and I grab Nova's spare without a thought.

Tossing it between my hands, I feel its weight pressing down. Twirling it between my fingers, I make my way to a practice dummy.

Not even thinking, I slam the staff into its side, knocking it to the floor. I turn around and send the dummy behind me flying.

"Why didn't you come to my room and figure things out with us, Nova? You left me on my own," I exclaim as my staff slams into another dummy. Whirling around I bury the staff into the soft chest of a dummy and fall to my knees. So much for being strong.

"Damn it, Nova. Damn it. Why did you have to go and get yourself captured? I can't go on without you." Once again, I place my head against my hands as my back shakes with sobs. "I love you, Nova. I freaking love you and I'm sorry I didn't admit it earlier. I thought I was protecting you but I should have told you."

I can almost feel my hearts breaking because deep down I know the chances of getting him back are slim to none. I'm going to regret every second I spent arguing with him, every time we spoke and I didn't say I loved him, every second I remember I could have gone with him.

I can hope we will be able to rescue him before he dies.

Chapter Twenty-nine

Ara

"Somehow, I knew we would find you down here," I hear Seginus say.

I glance up and see him and Pandra slowly approaching me as I sit here on the floor of the training center. They drop down to the floor next to me.

"Looks like you were having all the fun without us," Pandra laughs.

"Did you have to completely destroy all the practice dummies?" he asks motioning to the targets and dummies I left on the floor or falling apart due to me shredding them with my staff.

I snicker at his comment. "They deserved it. Like every Constable I lay my hands on when we go on that mission, they all deserve to suffer and die for what they have done."

"I can second that," Pandra nods. "They all deserve to die."

Seginus glances over at me. "Are you sure you are okay? You have been much more violent ever since..."

"Don't even say his name," I growl, interrupting him. Not wanting to even think about what could be happening to Nova right now.

"Alright."

We sit in silence for a while. The sound of our soft breaths could be heard in the large training room.

I say I don't want to think about him but deep down, I have to wonder. Maybe, maybe I could talk to Seginus and Pandra.

"He meant every word he told you," Seginus says suddenly.

"About what?" I ask, confused as to what he was referring to.

"About how he loves you," he answers.

"He did," Pandra agrees, "Everyone could see it but you two."

173

"Oh," is all I reply, of all the things they could bring up, it had to be that.

"He promised to himself he would protect you. He loved you, Ara. I don't know if you realized that, but he loved you," Seginus sighs.

"I love him too but he never saw it," I whisper.

"You do?" he asks, surprised.

"Yes, why do you think I have hung around him for this long? Most can't last a day because of his temper, although through this war it has gotten much worse. People are scared of him, but I'm not. He seemed like he was always on edge...and now I understand why," I explain.

Seginus nods. "When we find him, you need to talk. There are many things both of you must clear up with each other or else it may never happen."

"What do you think they will do to him?" I ask softly, not looking over to see Seginus' reaction.

"Do you want me to be honest or do you want me to tell you what you want to hear?" he asks.

"I want you to be honest. There is no point in trying to soften the blows anymore, war is relentless and I have to get used to it," I sigh.

"To be honest, I can guess at what they have planned. They could torture him to get information, they could force him to fight or they could kill him. However, since they came all this way and didn't kill him on sight here, I think they need him for some reason," Seginus answers.

Pandra puts an arm around me, but I push her off. Right now, all I want is Nova, but I know I can't have him.

I nod. "That's what I figured. The Council is planning something, with him at the center of it all. Which scares me."

"It scares me too," Seginus agrees. "The one thing we can do about it now is try to get him and the other hybrids back. In the meantime, the rebels want to see what their new leader has to say about events that have happened recently."

"I have to make speeches? No one told me that was in the job description," I gasp.

Pandra rolls her eyes. "It's not that hard."

Seginus laughs as he stands, beckoning me to follow him out of the training center. I glare at the back of his head as I follow behind him. I don't think I have recovered enough from Nova's kidnapping to talk to the entire rebel force. However, I don't think I have a choice.

He leads me outside, and my breath gets caught in my throat at the sight of the rebel force gathered at the bottom of the hill. They all seem to stare at me, how am I supposed to give them hope when I don't even have any of my own?

"Draw your staff and look strong. We rebels will not take a weak leader," Seginus instructs softly.

I pull my staff...Nova's staff, from it holster across my back. I slam it into the ground, the sound echoing, silencing the force.

"We have lost many today. However, we won. We won this battle, and a war is won battle by battle. I thank you for fighting a fight that was not originally yours. With your help, we will ensure the Council and Zubenelgenubi never rule Ode again and we become a peaceful planet once more." I glance around as I speak.

The people cheer in agreement.

"So, we fight. We will win this war. We will avenge our lost leaders and gain back our world." I thrust the staff into the air as it fills with the sounds of cheers. I look to Seginus and he nods, indicating I did what was needed.

I may not have given them hope, but I made sure they wanted to win this war more than anything.

"Ara, there are a few more things I need to speak with you about," Seginus says as he follows me into the building.

I turn to him. "What else could I possibly need to know about?"

"It's about the Council and Zubenelgenubi," he sighs, continuing to follow me as I walk.

"It's always about them." I roll my eyes.

"They know you are alive."

"What?" I can't believe they would know. I can't seem to take another step. This news practically bolts my feet to the floor.

"They know. We had a mole that leaked the information back to the Council. It has been taken care of now, but we must act soon. They have Nova, and they will use him to get to the rebels and you," Seginus explains.

"W-we must act quickly then," I stutter, my head suddenly reeling. "Plans must be finalized."

He nods in agreement, "Then let's go. We don't have long until the executions."

Moments later we are back in the control center. I hit the button on the hologram table and it lights up.

Nova left everything there was to know about the plans for us. He must have somehow known I would take over if something were to happen to him. He always did like to plan ahead.

"Do we have the coordinates of the arsenal we are to raid?" I ask Seginus, not taking my eyes away from the files I had been reading.

"We do," he answers from the other side of the table, where he too searches for whatever information he can find.

"Good, our entire plan depends on us being able to raid that arsenal. Do we have enough H.P.V.'s to carry the force?" I question, not wanting to tire everyone out by having them walk the entire way.

"I have already called for the rest of the fleet."

I nod, so far everything should be alright. "I will go in with the second team. I want to see the Council and Zubenelgenubi for myself."

"Then I will go with you," Seginus says.

"No," I shake my head, "You need to lead the rest of the force."

"Ara, I promised Nova, that if anything happened to him I would make sure you survived this. I will not go back on my word now. I am going with you whether you like it or not. It was Nova's wish." Seginus looks up at me, his mouth set in a firm line.

I sigh in defeat. "Fine."

I should have known Nova would do something like that.

"Then the plans have been set. Once the force has gotten some rest we will begin. The attack will directly follow the raid. We may throw them off with the element of surprise," he says.

"Let's hope that it will," I agree.

Chapter Thirty

In the Council Dwellings

"Sir?" A voice brings Zubenelgenubi out of his thoughts.

"What?" he snaps, shifting on his throne.

"They have caught Lieutenant Stargazer," the Council member says.

Zubenelgenubi smiles. "Send for my brother and bring Stargazer in, I want to see him."

The Council member nods and leaves the room, returning moments later with Zubeneschamali.

"Have you heard the good news brother? The have brought in Stargazer. I have instructed that he be brought here before being thrown in a cell. I would like to see what he has to say about the rebels," Zubenelgenubi laughs as he beckons his brother to stand next to his throne.

The moment his brother stands next to him the doors open, and two Constables drag in the limp body of Nova Stargazer. They throw him to the floor where he lays unmoving.

"He should wake up here in a moment," one Constable says as he steps back.

A low groan echoes through the room as Nova shifts, the drug quickly wearing off. Nova lays there dazed for a moment before jumping to his feet and quickly looking around the room.

Zubenelgenubi grins and stands from his throne, walking slowly down to Nova. "Lieutenant Stargazer how nice it is to finally see you again."

"Zubenelgenubi, Zubeneschamali, I see you two are still up to your old tricks. Say, I didn't think either of you made it through training. Is that why you sit on a throne that doesn't belong to you like a coward?" Nova sneers.

Zubenelgenubi huffs. "You are the reason we were kicked out of the force if I do remember correctly."

Nova rolls his eyes, "What do you want? Why am I here?"

"You are here because you are going to end this war," Zubeneschamali answers, walking up and joining his brother.

"Oh, I'm going to end it alright," Nova nods, stepping toward the two brothers, "After I kill both of you."

The two Constables pull him back, holding him a safe distance from the leaders. Zubenelgenubi laughs. "You will be killing. However, I will leave that part to General Vanil," he smirks. "For now, I want to find out how much you know about the rebels."

Nova is silent, his face set in a grim frown.

"You must know something. You were their leader after all," Zubeneschamali presses.

"I will tell you nothing," Nova growls.

"Fine, take him to his cell." Zubenelgenubi turns and walks back to his throne.

Nova struggles against the Constables. One draws his staff, slamming the end into the side of Nova's head. He crumples immediately, and they drag him away.

"Such a shame that we have to force him to fight for us," Zubeneschamali sighs as he stands next to his brother.

"It is. It would be easier to get information, but we have him now. The rebels will not be able to do very much," his brother says.

"Let us hope, for the sake of this war, they won't," Zubeneschamali purses his lips, genuinely afraid of what the rebels planned as revenge.

Chapter Thirty-one

Nova

What have I done? I let them take me. Why didn't I fight back? Why didn't I protect her? Why didn't I stay down there with her, like she asked me to? None of this would have happened. I would still have her. She would still be safe. Oh gosh, what have I done? I practically left the love of my life alone to freaking die. I don't even know if she is still at the base or if she was also captured. Wait, what if she's here?

My eyes shoot open, and I quickly look around the room they put me in after I tried to assault their leaders. My heart s sink when I realize she isn't here. I should be glad she isn't here. That means there is a higher chance she escaped, but she also might be in another room, and who knows what they could be doing to her.

I stand up. I need to find out if she is here. If she is then I need to help her escape. I can't risk them killing her. She is the last hybrid, and I'm not going to let the Council kill her.

I walk over to the door and press the button again and again. It doesn't open no matter how many times I slam my fist into the button. Why would it? I'm a prisoner, and they wouldn't enable the door to open unless someone else was in here.

Dang, it, how the heck am I going to get out of here? I glance around the room again. There are no windows and no other doors.

Suddenly the door opens, and I whip around.

Oh no. This is not good.

"Look who we have here. The infamous Nova Stargazer."

"General Vanil," I sigh.

Great, this is exactly who I wanted to see. In other words,

I'm screwed.

"So Nova, are the rumors I have been hearing true? That you have taken it up with a hybrid girl? What did they say her name was again? A...A...Ara? Was that it?" General Vanil asks.

"Where is she? Take me to her. If she's hurt I swear I will kill someone," I start toward him.

Two other Constables hold me back.

"I'll take that as a yes. As far as I know she is fine, back at your rebel base with our spy," he says as he walks around me.

"I knew there was a spy," I mutter.

"Oh yes, and she's quite good. She has yet to even be suspected, I'm very proud of her," The General grins.

"Who is it?" I growl. I need to know if Ara is in immediate danger.

"All I can say is the one hybrid we haven't gotten to is Ara," he turns away from me for a moment.

I need to get out of here and get back to Ara now!

"See I've been meaning to ask you a question Nova, and now that I have the chance, I think I will. Why did you quit? You were the best Constable we ever had, and you were on your way to taking my place," he asks as his cruel silver eyes stare at me.

"I quit because I didn't believe what we were doing was right," I answer.

"For some reason, I don't think that is why. I think you quit because of her. I think you quit because you were afraid she would think you were a monster and would never love you. Is that the reason?" Vanil comes closer, his height equal with mine.

My hearts sink. There is no reason to keep up the act anymore.

"Your face tells it all. You must be completely smitten with her. What is it? Her bright silver eyes? Her long silky hair? How about her lips? Soft sweet tasting lips?" he questions as he steps closer.

"It should not matter what she looks like. I have a few words. Just because she is a hybrid does not mean you have to hunt her down," I respond.

"That's why you have to kill her," he says.

My head snaps up, "What?"

"You have to kill her," he repeats.

"I-I can't. I could never kill her out of cold blood," I gasp.

"If you can't do it, I know who can. Pin him down, boys," Vanil orders.

The two Constables push me to the ground and hold down my arms and legs.

No, not the trigger. They can't use the trigger.

One of the two Constables rips open my shirt, revealing the scars from when I joined the Constables, Κυνῆγός, Greek for hunter. The raised letters branded on my upper chest.

"Get the other brand," Vanil instructs.

One Constable leaves the room for a moment and returns with the red-hot brand.

"Please," I beg. "You don't have to do this."

General Vanil grins. "Oh but I do. I know how you think Stargazer. You will promise to do something, but the second we turn you loose you will turn on us. The trigger is the only way to make sure you do as I say. That is why all Constables are forced to have one."

The Constable hands him the brand, still red-hot.

"Please, Vanil," I beg as I struggle, trying to escape the grips of the Constables who hold me down. My eyes follow the brand as it inches closer, "No, No."

The sudden pain is unbearable as a new word is burned into my skin next to the one that was already there.

Then the world fades away into black.

~ * ~

"Sir, why am I being held down?"

"Stand up, Lieutenant Stargazer," Vanil orders.

I stand. "What are my orders?"

"Your orders are to kill the hybrid girl that goes by the name Ara."

Chapter Thirty-two

Ara

"The fleet has arrived," Seginus says as he steps into the control room.

I look up from the map I had been studying, a map of the Council dwellings to be exact. "Have you prepared the troops?" I ask, turning off the hologram table and walking towards Seginus.

"I have," he answers as he hands me my staff in its holster, which had at one time belonged to Nova. I slip it over my head and adjust the strap going across my chest and around to the actual holster in the back.

Seginus then hands me my cloak, a black one as dark as a night without stars. I tie it around my shoulders as I step out of the control center.

"Are you ready?" he asks, pressing the button and closing the door.

I nod, "I believe I am."

"Then let's get going."

Our footsteps pad down the empty hallways. Every person capable of fighting or contributing is coming along. We can use as much help as we can get.

The moment I step into the hangar full of H.P.V.s and rebels it goes silent. Everyone's eyes rest on me, expecting me to give them words of courage.

I glance around at the faces, humans, Oderians and Pandra, the last other hybrid left free, standing side by side. "I am going, to be honest with all of you," my voice echoes bouncing back and forth from wall to wall in the hanger. "This may be suicide mission. If we fail, that's it. The rebels will be no more. The Council now knows the locations of two of our bases. It will only be a matter of time before they find the rest. If the mission succeeds, even though the chances are slim, we will forever change Ode.

Let us make our world a better place, but first, let Ode fall into rebellion."

The rebels cheer, and the sound is deafening. No one seems to care that most of the people around them will fall on this mission.

Lines form as everyone boards the ships to their ultimate demise. I shake my head, wiping the morbid thought from my mind. I have to focus on getting through this and saving Nova. Even if it means abandoning the mission once I find him.

I feel the H.P.V. rumble beneath us and rise into the air.

"How long will it take the fleet to make it to the arsenal?" I ask, turning to Seginus.

"Not long, we will be traveling at top speed. The quicker we are there the less likely we will raise any alarms," he says, glancing over at my concerned expression.

"Good," I nod.

The flight was smooth for a while as we all sat in silence, trying not to imagine the horrors that await us when we land. Pandra gives me a few sympathetic glances, but I ignore them. My thoughts are on getting to Nova, no matter what.

I jump when the H.P.V. begins shaking. A loud explosion sounds outside. I stand and pull a door open, revealing the pilot.

"What's happening?" I yell over the sound of another explosion as the ship trembles in the air.

"The Council is trying to shoot us out of the sky," the pilot answers.

I groan sarcastically, "Wonderful."

"What do you expect me to do about it?" he snaps.

"Shoot back," I exclaim, "And tell the other ships to do the same. We can't get shot out of the sky. We have a mission to complete."

I slam the door closed as another shot barely misses the ship and explodes.

Suddenly, I hear the pilot yell from the other side of the door. "What now?" I growl at him.

"We've lost three ships, and two have been hit," he answers

frantically.

"Where's your com unit?" I hiss, sick of putting up with him.

He shakily points to a small button next to him. I jab my finger onto it, "This is your leader speaking about the projectiles currently being shot at us. In order to solve this problem, I need you to shoot back. Shoot back, you idiots. Shoot back."

The pilot sits there quivering in his seat, eyes fixed on me. "Fly the damn ship," I sneer. I am not going to deal with this today, of all days.

He jerks his head back toward the front, to focus on flying and taking out whatever was shooting at us.

I step through the small door, and everyone stares at me. I quickly realize I left the door open. My entire team heard the whole exchange.

"Today is not the day to be cowards, so if you plan to be one I'd advise that you get off this ship right now," I huff as their faces pale.

I drop back down into the seat next to Seginus. He looks at me surprised. "Was that really necessary?"

I nod. "Yes it was. No one can afford to be cowardly today, not even me. So today, I am not opposed to speaking my mind."

He shrugs. "As long as the mission is completed."

"As long as the mission is completed," I repeat half-heartedly.

The ship shivers in the air again as another explosion rings in our ears. "I swear, I'm going to have to start killing Constables to let off some steam," I groan.

"I thought we all did that," Pandra snorts.

I glare at her. "Don't push it."

She shakes her head. "Alright, alright."

I give Seginus a slight nudge as I feel the ship began to sink to the ground. "We are here."

I stand along with my team, the doors opening the moment the ship touches the ground. I give a slight nod, and we all unload.

My team pulls together into a tight formation, "Remember." I say to them softly, "We came for the weapons we can use in the upcoming battle. Also, if you run into any Constables, and it's likely that we will, kill them. Show no mercy to those who have killed our families."

My team, followed by a few other teams, slowly makes our way into the large building. I draw my staff, prepared for anything that could be hiding around the next corner.

After clearing several hallways, we find the armory. It has been too quiet this whole mission. Something is wrong. Something is very wrong.

"Be ready," I whisper to my team. "This could be a trap."

Seginus nods in agreement. We line up along the wall, preparing to open up the door. I motion for him to go on.

He slams his fist into the control panel, and the door slides open. Suddenly, an alarm starts to blare. "We need to hurry," I exclaim, quickly stepping through the door. "Grab as much as you can then let's get out of here."

The teams shove whatever weapons they can into their bags. Seginus and I stand guard inside the room, giving both of us a slightly better sense of safety.

Everyone lines back up once they can no longer hold anything else. I start to leave the room but freeze when I hear the sound of boots marching down the hall.

I glance to Seginus, who nods indicating that he also heard them.

"Get ready to fight," I whisper softly to my team.

The moment the first few Constables step into the room, we pounce and they fall to the floor rather quickly. They flood into the room, and chaos breaks out. Constables thrust their staves, and the rebels deflect them, landing deathly blows as quickly as they can.

If we had gotten out of here faster, we would not have had to deal with all these Constables. In a fit of rage, my fist snags a Constable's cloak, and I slam him against the wall.

He groans in pain as I let out a growl. "This is what you get for coming after the rebels." Without even thinking I shatter the globe on my staff and run him through with it. He slides down the wall leaving streaks of purple blood.

I wipe my staff off with his cloak and turn to find everyone staring at me and what I had done. I give them a glare and hiss, "Let's get out of here before I have to do that again."

The teams straighten up and follow Seginus and me out of the room, loaded down with everything we could possibly grab. However, I spoke far too soon.

Once more we hear the thumps of boots coming down the hall.

"I'll deal with this," I whisper as I motion for the team to take the alternate route out.

I glance back to see that everyone had left but Seginus and Pandra.

"Get going you two," I sigh.

"No," they both reply.

I shrug. "Alright then."

Suddenly, the Constables round the corner. However, the one in the front center looks different from the rest. Instead of the usually dark blue Constable uniform, his is deep red.

They stop and the Oderian in red stares at me.

"Arrest them," he orders.

The Constables behind him race forward before I even have the chance to draw my staff. Two hold Seginus and me back, one on each side of both of us.

"Good job, now come here," he says, his expression unchanging.

"What?" I ask, confused.

Pandra walks right up to him, and nods. "General Vanil."

"What's going on?" Seginus asks as he moves to stand next to me.

"It's quite simple really. You two made the mistake of trusting a spy," the General laughs.

My gaze sets itself on Pandra. "How could you?" I hiss.

She shrugs.

"You betrayed me. You betrayed my trust. How much have you told them?" I gasp.

"Oh, she's told us everything," he grins.

"Why, Pandra?" I cry, as I struggle against the two Constables. "Why would you betray your race?"

Once again, she shrugs.

"I want to know, now," I growl.

"It's so much more fun to manipulate people. Like I said when I first met you, I love getting into people's heads. Especially Nova's, messing with him was the most fun I've ever had," she grins. Her entire demeanor has changed.

"You see, Ara, I asked her to bring you to me and that's exactly what she did." General Vanil leans against the wall.

I shake my head, "He's using you Pandra, once this is all done and you are of no more use to him, he will kill you."

Pandra's expression doesn't change.

"You see..." The General trails off, a sly smile playing at his lips. "It's come quicker than I thought."

Suddenly a Constable throws him his staff.

"Watch out," I exclaim, but I'm too late.

Pandra turns as General Vanil runs the staff right through her stomach.

"No," I scream.

Seginus watches, too horrified to speak as Pandra crumples to her knees.

"You promised," she breathes looking up at the General.

He spits at her, "I lied, you filthy hybrid."

Something inside me kicks on and I manage to rip myself from the Constable's grip. In mere seconds the two that were holding me back, along with the two who were holding Seginus back, lay dead on the floor.

I turn back around so I can go after the General next, but find he is gone.

Pandra falls the rest of the way to the floor, clawing at the staff embedded inside her.

"Pandra," I sigh as I sit down next to her while Seginus stands guard.

"I'm sorry," she groans. "He said he would let me live."

"You still lied. If you had told us, we could have helped you," I say.

She shakes her head, "No. Nothing could have helped me."

She starts to cough up blood, making the pool she lies in ever larger. "I am truly sorry." Her regenerative shock kicks in, and she continues to breathe for a few moments before she stops.

Seginus hands me a glass vial, and I catch her silver tears.

"I can't believe she was the mole," I whisper.

"Neither can I," Seginus agrees.

I glance down at my once best friend one last time as I stand up.

"I truly am the last one," I choke as I try to hold back tears.

Seginus sets his hand on my back. "So, let's end this. Come on. We need to leave before General Vanil returns with more Constables."

We weave our way back through the halls and meet with the other teams outside the arsenal.

"Did you leave any Constable survivors?" I ask their leaders as I try to push Pandra from my mind.

They shake their heads, telling me that no one was left alive. Suddenly, it makes me regret Pandra's death even more. I shake it off, trying desperately to find any way to justify me just letting her die. She deserved it. She was a spy, and she was the reason so many died in the attacks on the bases. She deserved it.

I nod. "Good."

I ordered we spare the innocents and kill everyone else. Any Constables left alive could jeopardize us later on. It also gives the Council a smaller force to call in for backup.

Everyone quickly loads back onto the H.P.V.s. Now, we go to the Council dwellings where we will end this terrible war.

The Council continues to try and shoot us out of the sky as we fly. The explosions are deafening, and the ship continually shakes and trembles in the sky.

I stumble up to the door to the pilot and hit the panel to open it. "Land here and tell the other ships to do the same. Then take back to the sky to continue the aerial assault."

"We are still a long way from the dwellings..." the pilot argues.

"I don't care. Land the ship, and tell the others to do the same."

He lands the ship moments later. I assemble the rebel troops as the H.P.V.s rise back into the sky.

We start our march to the dwellings. Many thoughts cross my mind as we walk to our possible doom. The Council could know we are coming for them. We could easily be walking into a trap. They could have some secret weapon they plan to use against us, or then again, they may have already been informed of our incoming attack.

The explosions of bombs get louder as we draw near the dwellings. The sky begins to grow dark as the troops prepare themselves for the battle that will happen at first light.

Chapter Thirty-three

Ara

"Let's go," I shout over another explosion. They continued throughout the night, lighting up the sky enough for me to be able to see.

For some reason, my glow shut itself off again after what happened at the base when Nova was taken, and I am left in the cold dark.

Since the raid on the arsenal went exactly as planned, the rebels are stocked on weapons. Overnight, teams went in one by one and took down as many Constables under the cover of darkness as they could. The path into the dwelling had easily been cleared, so now the one job left to be done is for me and my team to take out what remains of the Council and the Council leaders.

I previously received information from an operative saying Nova was sentenced to be hung along with many hybrids. The executions are going to start soon. I can hope we will be able to get to them before they are all dead. My worst fear is they will speed up the process before we have a chance to save them or the information was not true in the first place.

The group I am leading is the one that will go in and rescue the hybrids. Taking out the Council will be the next step. I plan to break off and find Nova. There is so much I need to tell him.

My team and I weave our way to the dwellings on high alert even though the area was cleared last night. There could still be some Constables hiding and waiting to ambush us. We carefully watch our backs, knowing they like to sneak up on people and take them out before they even have a chance to scream out for help.

"Oh no," I breathe as we approach the dwellings. "We are too late."

The gallows stand just below the steps and are littered with bodies. All the hybrids we were here to save are now dead. They must have sped up the executions knowing we were coming.

I avert my eyes, not wanting to look at the bodies anymore. There are too many.

We approach the entrance to the dwellings and start to climb the first flight of steps. I glance up and see a figure at the top of the second flight.

I motion for the team to stop and call up to the person, "If you are a Constable, surrender. There is no point in fighting back now. The winner of this war has already been decided."

The person starts down the steps slowly, and I squint up at him. After a few seconds, I recognize the person. My hearts leap to my throat, and I completely forget my position of authority.

"Nova," I exclaim. I rush up the stairs to him. "You're alive!" My hands cup his cheeks as I speak, "There is something very important I need to speak to you about after we win this war." I throw my arms around his neck and hug him tightly. "I am so glad you are alive. I'm sorry we didn't come sooner."

Suddenly, he shoves me away and draws his staff. I stumble back as he taps the globe on the ground and it shatters, its sharp, jagged pieces gleaming in the light. Then he points it at me.

"Nova? What are you doing?" I ask as I carefully draw my own staff and hold it up in a defensive position. A thought nags at the back of my head. Nova would never do something like this at such an unprecedented time.

He quickly takes a step forward, lunging toward me, aiming for my chest. I block the attack, shoving his staff aside and take another step back.

"Nova, this isn't the time for a practice fight," I gasp as I block another attack.

Something is wrong. He has never been this hard on me. He has never had the look he gets when trying to kill someone when he is battling me.

I take another step back and block another attack.

"Nova? What's wrong? What did I do?" I ask.

He stays silent as I block another attack, and this time I

shove him back with the butt of my staff. He lifts up his staff and catches my arm with it, slashing my bare skin.

I hiss in pain, and purple blood drips from the cut.

"You're not pure. You must die," he growls.

I glance up at his silver eyes. They look clouded and distant. This isn't my Nova, he is different. He will not hesitate to kill me. This is the side of himself he warned me about in the cave, the side this war alone could bring out of him. The Council must have done this.

His attacks get quicker, and I start to have a harder time blocking them. He may have trained me, but he still has moons more experience than I do. He is going to kill me if I don't do something.

Suddenly something takes over, and I slip in an attack, shoving him backward. He recovers quickly and tackles me to the ground.

"Nova, stop," I groan under his weight.

He sits up, keeping me pinned to the ground with his legs and pointing his staff at my chest. He lifts it up, about to impale me with it.

Somehow, I get the strength to shove him off me, his staff rolling away. He regains his feet quickly and dives for his staff. As I stand, I tap the globe I replaced last night after killing the Constable on the ground, and it shatters.

He is going to kill me. I need to do something. I watch as he lifts his staff, preparing for the kill. He runs at me and without thinking, I bury the sharp remains of the globe into his chest.

Time seems to slow down. My hearts feel like they have stopped in my chest and his staff clatters to the ground as I realize what I have done. I pull out my staff and stare at it for a moment. Nova's blood shimmers and drips from its tip.

He stares at his chest as his clothes start to turn purple from his blood. He stumbles toward me and his silver eyes seem to clear. A knot forms in my stomach.

"Ara?" he gasps as I catch him in my arms.

"I'm sorry, I'm sorry. I-I didn't mean to…" I cry out as tears start to well up in my eyes.

What have I done?

I carefully lower Nova to the ground and tear his stained shirt down the middle so I can look at the wound. My hearts ache for it to not be as bad as I imagine.

As I study it, I realize the globe pierced two of his hearts. It is as bad as I thought it was. He is going to die. I don't understand why he hasn't gone into regenerative shock yet.

My hands tremble as I look up at his face. I feel tears sliding down my cheeks and drip, landing on his chest.

"N-Nova, you're going to…" I falter, unable to even comprehend what is happening.

"I'm going to die," he finishes in a raspy voice.

I glance down at his chest, his shirt ripped open. I notice a fresh burn. A word, branded across his chest next to one that looks much older. *Υπακούω* it reads, Greek for obey.

"It's the trigger," he breathes. "How they got me to do what they wanted me to do." He lets out a hiss in pain. I tear a large portion of his shirt off and press it to his wound, trying to stop the bleeding.

"Nova, I'm sorry. I didn't mean to…"

"It's okay. I would have killed you if you hadn't. It was a kill or be killed situation," he interrupts.

I suck in a trembling breath. "I don't know what I'm going to do without you. You've been there for me my entire life. I love you for goodness sake."

His silver eyes seem to light up. "You have no idea how much I've wanted to hear those words from you."

"R-really?" I stutter through my tears.

He barely nods.

Chapter Thirty-four

Nova

I try to ignore the pain as I stare into Ara's eyes. They bring back so many memories of happiness.

~ * ~

"How long have we been up here?" Ara asks, pulling her gaze away from the stars above us.

I shrug, "I'm not really sure."

"You never know anything do you?" she laughs.

I smile. I live to hear that sound.

"Nope," I answer.

We both fall silent for a few minutes. I have found the two of us are as comfortable sitting in silence as we are talking back and forth.

I lay back, unable to sit up anymore. Ara still sits next to me, her gaze never leaving the stars. On a whim, I move slightly and set my head in her lap.

She looks down at me and smiles. One hand finds its way into my hair, the other sits on my chest.

The feeling of her fingers combing through my hair sends shivers down my spine. I don't have to smile for her to know that I am happy. The feeling of her next to me can calm me.

We sit there, our gazes interlocked and unwavering, lost in each other's eyes.

A smile plays at her lips as she continues to run her fingers along my scalp and forehead. I don't think I have ever seen her happier.

~ * ~

"Of all the Constable bases you could have chosen, you had to choose this one," Ara grumbles as we slip into the building.

"Shh, or we will be caught," I whisper to her.

I draw my staff as we stop at the corner and I peek around. I see no Constables so I motion for Ara to follow me into the room.

Their control room is covered in flashing monitors.

"I don't need very long Ara, all I need is enough time to download a few things," I say as I turn on their hologram table and swipe at a few files.

Ara walks around the room slowly, taking in every inch.

Suddenly she yells, "Nova, duck."

I drop to the floor and her staff goes flying right over my head followed by a loud thump.

She comes over to me quickly, "Are you alright?"

I nod. Turning, I find a Constable lying in a quickly growing pool of blood.

"What happened?" I ask.

"He came up behind you. If I hadn't of thrown my staff, you would be bleeding out right now," Ara answers. "Let's get out of here before one of us ends up dead."

She steps over the dead Constable's body, pulling her staff from his chest and makes her way out of the base with me on her tail.

"Thank you for saving my life, Ara."

She looks back at me and grins, "My how the tables have turned, for once you are indebted to me."

"Don't let it go to your head," I laugh.

~ * ~

"Nova," Ara screams as the Constable's staff catches my side. The long gash quickly starts oozing blood.

"I'm fine, stay back."

For the moment I ignore it, and continue fighting, knowing if I let my guard down again there will be more than a long gash on my body.

I block attack after attack until I finally find an opening. I quickly slam my staff into the side of the Constable's head, and he falls to the ground, dead.

Suddenly the world starts to spin, and I drop to my knees.

"Nova," Ara exclaims again.

She comes running over, dropping to her knees in front of me and soon her hands find their way to my cheeks.

"Are you alright?" I breathe, trying not to let the pain show in my voice.

She shakes her head. "I'm fine. You, on the other hand, have lost a lot of blood."

"Have I?" I ask. The pain seems to be getting worse. I glance down and the purple pool beside me makes my head spin. "I guess I have."

"Come on, you'll die if we don't get that bandaged up," she says.

Ara slips her shoulders under my arm and helps me to my feet. I groan in pain. She glances at me frowning.

"Back to the H.P.V.," she states.

I stumble back with Ara's help.

By the time we actually make it back black spots start to appear in my vision. Ara helps me lie down on the floor of the H.P.V.

"I need to wrap that quickly. You have already lost far too much blood," Ara sighs. "Lift your tunic up."

I barely nod as she pulls the tunic up just enough to get a better look at the wound on my lower side. All I see is a deep frown settle upon her face.

"What is it?" I breathe.

"It's bad," she shakes her head. "I have to clean it then wrap it."

She bends down, carefully dabbing at the blood, soaking it up and wiping away any dirt to keep the wound from being infected.

Ara leans closer as she wraps the bandages around my side. I hiss in pain as she pulls them tight.

"Sorry," she frowns again as she ties it off.

"Thank you," I say as I catch her hand in mine.

Our eyes lock, and we stay that way for a moment, eyes interlocked, hand in hand. Suddenly she pulls her hand out of mine and looks away.

"We need to go."

~ * ~

"Ara, you need to stop training and eat something," I state as I walk up behind her.

She continues to beat the practice dummy.

"Ara," I exclaim. I snatch the staff from her hands. "You have to give yourself a break."

She turns to me, "How can I? There are people out there dying for Pandra and me."

"They chose to do that," I sigh.

"But…" Ara closes her eyes.

"Are you alright?" I ask.

She sways slightly from side to side.

"Ara?"

Suddenly, she crumbles. I catch her before she hits the floor.

"Ara, wake up," I sigh as I kneel down, lowering her to the floor.

Her eyes slid open slowly, "What happened?"

"You collapsed. I told you to go eat, but you didn't listen." I roll my eyes.

"But…" She tries again.

"No, if you hurt yourself, what do those people have to fight for? Nothing. You have to take care of yourself so the people risking their lives will have a reason to do so."

Chapter Thirty-five

Ara

"Remember when we used to lay on the roof of your house?"

"I could never forget," I whisper.

"There were so many times when we were up there I wanted to tell you I love you, but I knew the Council would never allow it. I knew this was coming, and I'm sorry I didn't do anything more to stop this from happening," he groans, curling into his wound, trying to ease the pain as best he could.

His bloody hand presses against my cheek as I let out a sob.

"It will be alright, Ara. I'll be with the stars..." He bites his lip trying to push back and ignore the pain, "So when you look up at the stars, from your roof, know the light shining down is my glow, keeping you warm. Keeping you safe."

"Nova, please," I exclaim, "Please don't."

"I want you to do one last thing for me, Ara," he whispers, the light starting to fade from his eyes.

My tears seem to run rapids down my cheeks. "Anything, anything you want."

"End this war," he whispers.

I force a smile, nodding as I do so, "I will end it, I promise." I stroke his cheek. On a whim I lean down and press my lips to his. I sit back up slowly.

He smiles, "Goodbye, Ara."

"No," I sob as his eyes slide closed. "Nova, no, please. Please don't leave me. I need you, I need you to help me." My sobs interrupt my words. "Nova!" I scream, shaking his shoulders like it would pull him out of the arms of death that were dragging him away. "Nova," I cry as I hold him close, willing him to breathe again, to wake up.

Reaching into my cloak I pull out a small clear glass vial. I knew I would need one of these, but I never thought I would need one for Nova.

I watch as two small silver tears slide down his face in sync with my own. I catch them in the vial and plug it up and put it back into my cloak, next to my hearts.

I sit there holding him, rocking back and forth. Unable to figure out if I was crying for the loss of him or if I was crying because of the pain. The pain in my hearts doesn't fade. With the beat of each one it seems to grow more and more. I sob until my lungs hurt, until I can't stop shaking, until I have no more tears to cry but dry sobs rack my body.

I jump at the sound of a scream but then realize it was my own. Finally, I start to come back to my senses. I glance down at Nova as he lays motionless in my arms, his blood all over me. I gently set him down and fold his arms across his chest.

I stare down at his peaceful face and brush his soft brown hair out of the way. He lays there in a pool of his own blood. He didn't deserve to die like that.

Suddenly, I remember my own words. "His death will not be in vain."

"No, it will not," I mutter to myself as I stand. I glance back down at him and whisper, "This is for you."

I turn back to my teams, who stare at me, heartbroken by what they witnessed. I wouldn't blame them for that. "Let's end this."

I pick up my staff and head into the dwellings. The Council and its leaders are going to pay for Nova's death.

We stop in front of a large ornate door. "That is where the twins will be. We need to take them out first," Seginus says, stepping up next to me.

"I'm going to kill both of them," I growl. "They are the reason he is dead."

"Be careful. Nova trained both of them himself, so they will know every trick you know and more if they really want you dead, " Seginus whispers as I step up closer to the door listening to see if there was anyone inside.

I hear nothing, but that doesn't mean they aren't in the building.

I walk over to the control panel and press the button, hoping it hadn't been locked from the inside. The door opens the second I let go of the button.

I slowly step into the dark room, my anger rising with every breath I take. They will die knowing they killed someone who didn't deserve that fate.

My eyes fall on the glows of two Oderians on the other side of the room. They seem to be on a raised platform.

I move silently in the darkness, prepared for anything. "Do you call yourselves kings?" My voice rings out, echoing in the large room.

"Who's there?" one asks.

"It doesn't matter who I am. I asked you a question, do you call yourselves kings?" I growl, not in the mood to bicker after what happened.

"We like to think we are kings, kings of this world and kings of a pure race," one answers but with a slightly different voice, that must be the other twin.

"Do you know whose death you have caused?" I ask as I watch their confusion, still trying to figure out who had entered the room.

"We have caused many deaths, most of them were unimportant," the one sitting down says.

"Unimportant you say? You believe they didn't mean anything? They all had families. They all had people who loved them," I say, stepping closer to them in the darkness.

"They were not needed. They will not help make Ode the planet it is destined to become." He stands looking around the room, trying to find me.

"He was very important. He is someone who has helped Ode try to get rid of you, but in the end, he died before he got the chance, so I am here to finish his job," my voice gets louder as speak.

"Why can't we see you?" They continue to look for a glow in the darkness.

"Because I'm not like you, and I never will be. I will never be a murderer," I hiss.

"You are a hybrid," one exclaims.

"At last, you have figured it out," I sigh.

Suddenly the roof of the room begins to open, count on Seginus to add to the drama. Light streams into the room, first landing on me standing in the middle of the room.

"It's her," they gasp together.

"Of course, it's me, who else would be here?" I snicker.

"How are you not dead? General Vanil promised he would kill you then report back. Where is Stargazer?" The one dressed in the finer cloak starts down the steps of the platform.

"Nova is dead," I answer, drawing my staff.

"H-how?" he stutters.

"I killed him..." I pause. "No, actually you killed him. He is dead because you thought it would be a great idea to send him after me. You lost a good Constable today because of your insolence."

"You were not supposed to be good enough to have defeated him, besides you were close to him. It couldn't have been easy to murder him in cold blood," he takes another step.

"You know, I don't even know who you two are. All I know is you have taken over the Council," I grin mischievously.

"I am Zubenelgenubi," the one on the steps says.

"I am Zubeneschamali," the other answers.

"I do not doubt you also know who I am. I am the last known free hybrid. I am the leader of the rebels, and I am the lover of the now dead Nova Stargazer. I am many things," I pace, twirling my staff in my hand. They stare at me for a moment. "I am also the one who is going to free this planet of you. So, I will give you two choices."

"What are these choices?" Zubenelgenubi asks.

"You can both step away from the Council and disappear forever, or I can kill you here. It is your choice, but either way, you will no longer be able to run Ode," I explain.

They both nod. "I will also give you a choice. You can leave or we can call in our Constables," Zubeneschamali says.

I shake my head, "Do you think a bunch of Constables are going to be able to take me down now? Do you think they will be able to take down the entire rebel army? I have killed many Constables by now. If you do not choose, I will choose for you and you will not enjoy my choice." They continue to stand their ground. Zubeneschamali slightly moves his hand to touch the back of the throne. The second his hand moves away. A force of Constables comes streaming into the room from a hidden door.

"Capture her," Zubenelgenubi exclaims.

I hold my staff up. These Constables wear a slightly different uniform than the rest of the force. These must be the Constables who directly defend these two.

They swarm at me, cloaks flying and boots stomping. I move on instinct, thrusting and jabbing when needed, turning and sweeping my staff at their legs at other times.

They groan in pain as they fall to the floor. I hear the swish of a cloak behind me and turn a little too late. The staff slams into my knees, sending me to the floor. My staff slips out of my grasp.

The Constable grabs my hair and yanks up my head. His fist connects with my cheek. I glare up at him as I spit blood on his boots. What was left of Constables line up behind me, looking to the twins for their next order.

They smirk down at me. "That is where you belong, hybrid. Down on your knees for your kings. You should have taken our offer. When you left, we would have captured you and you would have lived in captivity, like the animal you are. However, you didn't and now we are going to have to put you down," Zubenelgenubi laughs.

"You think this is funny?" I ask. "You think it is funny that many of your people are dead? You think it's funny that he is dead?"

He nods. "I do in fact."

"You killed him," I scream. "You killed my Nova, and you will pay. You will pay with your life. All of you!" My chest heaves, and my hair flies around my face in crazy wisps as I struggle to free myself from the Constable's grip.

"My, my, the little hybrid has a temper," Zubeneschamali grins, coming down the steps.

I sneer as he comes closer to me. "Do you want to find out if I bite like the animal you think I am?"

His fingers trail across my cheek as I smirk up at him. Suddenly, I yank my arms free of the Constable and grab my staff, plunging it through his hearts.

He crumples to the floor as I look up at his brother. "The answer is yes. I do bite, and rather hard too."

Zubenelgenubi stares at me, completely speechless. Moments later the Constable's bodies lay strewn across the floor. Their leader still stares at me in horror.

"I'm going to kill you because you killed Nova and others, and I think as I do it, I'm going to tell you exactly how Nova died. So, on your last dying breath, you will know exactly what pain you put him in." I take several steps closer to him.

"After that trigger you used he was going insane trying to kill me. That insanity caused him to make mistakes and give me a chance. He ran at me." I stop in front of Zubenelgenubi, my staff clutched in my hand.

"I ran him through." I thrust my staff into his stomach as I pull him close, almost leaning against me. I pull my staff out of him and throw it aside. "I helped him to the ground." I step away as the Council leader falls to the floor, staring up at me and begging for mercy. "I watched him die."

I stand there as the light fades from Zubenelgenubi's eyes. "You are a monster," he breathes. The silver stains the floor in two puddles, joining his own blood.

"I may be a monster, but at least I am one for the right cause," I spit as I turn away.

My eyes land on Seginus and my team. They stare in amazement at the mass of Constables on the floor and the two leaders now lying dead.

"Is there something wrong?" I ask sternly as I come down the steps.

"Did you do all this by yourself?" Seginus asks, coming up

to me.

"There was no one else here with me, yes. I killed them all. Is there a problem with that?" I raise my eyebrows as I pick up my staff and wipe the blood off of it.

Seginus shakes his head, "No. No there is not."

I nod, "Good." I look to the group, "The two leaders of the Council are now dead. They will have no way to get organized. We strike the final blow now."

Chapter Thirty-six

Ara

I slam open the door of the Council room. They all jump in surprise. I don't think any of them expected us to get into the dwellings.

"Listen up," I exclaim.

My team files into the room and each one grabs a Council member.

I jump onto the table, "You're all finished running Ode. Your leaders are dead. No more Council, no more Constables. Ode is free and you're leaving."

"You can't kick us out," one Council member says.

I turn toward him and sneer, "Watch me."

"I will not stand for this. I will have you executed. You will pay for the crimes of killing our leaders," he screeches. "Kill her."

Two Constables jump onto the table and come after me.

I draw my staff and push one off the table. The other continues to come at me. I block his staff several times before I put some force behind my own. His staff goes flying across the room, and I slash at his upper body. He falls to the floor. I drop to my knees next to the other and plunge the staff into his chest.

Standing up, I give the Council member a hard glare. "Who's next?"

He steps back, shaking his head. The rebels lead him and the rest of the Council out of the room. I follow close behind.

As we emerge from the dwelling I see thousands of people gathering at the bottom of the steps. I glance over at Nova's still body. I take off my cloak and drape it over him.

I look back up, seeing someone come up the steps, another Constable from the looks of it. His face is set in a smug smile as he watches me hover over Nova's body.

"I see you are still alive," he says.

"The same goes for you," I say, staring up at his hard eyes, my hand inching towards my staff.

"I guess Zubenelgenubi and Zubeneschamali didn't get what they so deeply desired," he sighs.

An uneasy feeling arises. He is not here for a good reason.

"How would you know that?" I stand up from my kneeled position.

"You killed the leaders, did you not?" he asks.

"I did, and since you are on their side, I believe I will have to kill you too," I answer.

He laughs, "I doubt you can. You had that chance and let it slip out of your grasp. You will have to answer to your crimes. I am the last one, so I must execute you."

"I would like to see you try, General Vanil," I sneer, drawing my staff once again.

The sharp remains of the globe are stained in blood, Nova's blood and the blood of those who paid for his death.

The General draws his own staff. "This is a game to you, hybrid. The twins knew nothing of fighting. You don't have enough experience to defeat me."

"Watch me," I growl.

He pounces, the same way Nova does. I quickly figure out that his style is exactly like Nova's, he must have learned straight from the General himself.

Our staves bounce off of each other, and the crowd below us gasps. It must have been his plan to kill me in front of what was left of Ode's people, to break them beyond the point of repair watching the third rebel leader die in this war.

I am not going to let him get away with it. This will be his last fight.

He slashes at my leg and leaves a long gash. I scream in pain and collapse down to my knees. His staff swipes across my cheek, blood leaking out and dripping to the ground. I am going to have a scar there for the rest of my life.

"I told you little hybrid, you were no match for me. My student may have taught you, but he did not teach you nearly enough before his untimely death," he laughs as he snatches my staff from my hands.

My chest heaves as I try to stand up, but my legs give out and I drop back to the ground. There I stay unable to stand, unable to fight back. Where has my team gone? Where has Seginus gone?

General Vanil turns to the people crying out at the bottom of the steps, they are too afraid to stand up to him. "This is the last free hybrid. She held arms against the Council. Take her as an example of what will happen to anyone else who fights back against your leaders. You will suffer the greatest of losses. You will lose loved ones. We will cut you down and shame you in front of the rest of the planet. Then, we will kill you."

He turns back to me as I stare up at him. "Kill me if you like, but there are still rebels out there. They will take their revenge on you and the Council," I sneer.

"You have fought your last battle, hybrid. You have watched the rest of your kind die. There is no reason to be the last one living, no point in being the last of a race," he shakes his head.

"Nova died so I could help finish making Ode fall into rebellion. You should not have forced me to kill him, as your death would have been quick and painless coming from him. From me? Oh, you will be wishing you were already dead," I hiss, my eyes landing on someone coming up behind him very slowly and quietly.

The General calls up one of his Constables and motions for him to hold me still. He yanks my arms behind me, forcing me to arch my back and then turns me to the crowd below. A chorus of shouts and protests echo. The General stands next to me, preparing his staff. He holds it over me, ready to plunge it through my hearts.

As he starts to move, he doubles over in pain, and I see Seginus standing behind him with his staff covered in blood. The Constable stands there wide-eyed and afraid. I throw a punch and hit him square in the jaw. There's a sickening crack, and he falls to the ground. I shake my hand out, wincing in pain. Maybe I should have grabbed a staff and used that to knock him out.

I turn to Seginus who stares at the motionless body of Nova. "We did it," I whisper to him.

Seginus nods, "We did. Nova would be very proud of you."

I glance up at the sky. "I would hope so."

I purse my lips, however, there is still much that has to be done. I look down at the crowd that stares up at us in awe. I motion to the dwellings. "The Council is finished," I exclaim.

Everyone cheers. The sound dies down a few moments later, and I speak again, "It was not without a price. We lost many good people, hybrid, Oderian, and human. Their deaths will not be in vain. We will rebuild Ode and remember those we lost."

Everyone cheers again.

"Your death will not be in vain, Nova." The sky is starting to darken as night falls. The first night where no one is living in fear of the Council. My first night as a truly free hybrid. My first night without Nova here with me.

Chapter Thirty-seven

Ara

I am first to follow behind them. Four rebels, including Seginus, carry the platform Nova is laid out on. Others follow behind me, the silent procession draped in white. The dress that I'm in for Nova floats behind me.

I glance at Seginus, his words echoing in my ears. "You will lead the procession because you are the last person left alive who knew him decently."

Seginus was kind enough to plan everything so I wouldn't have to. I wanted Nova to be honored as a hero. A small temple was built for him. He would have been laid to rest in the bigger temple with everyone else who died during the war had I not spoken up.

I leave my thoughts as my gaze lands on the temple. It may be small, but I know Nova wouldn't want something extravagant. He probably wouldn't have even wanted his own temple. However, he needs to be honored for what he did for Ode.

I walk around Seginus and the other four, opening the doors to the temple for them. They carry Nova in and set down the platform.

"We will leave you alone for as long as you need," Seginus breathes.

"Thank you," I whisper as I watch them leave.

An eerie silence falls in the room. All I can hear is the sound of my soft breaths. I avoided looking at Nova, for fear I wouldn't be able to continue with the rest of the ceremony. Now, I force myself to look down.

This is actually the first time I have ever seen Nova clad

only in white. On Ode white is the symbol of death and peace. His cloak pools on the floor on either side of the platform, lying splayed out underneath him.

My eyes trail up to his face, his once silver eyes are closed, giving the illusion he is in his dream state.

I quickly look away unable to see him this way for much longer. I glance around the room. The room is dark and holographic images of stars float around us. Both his body and mind are now with the stars as he promised.

"Nova," I whisper, knowing he probably can't hear me from wherever he is. "Thank you so much for everything you did for me. You sacrificed yourself by becoming a Constable to protect me, knowing how I would feel later on about it. You sacrificed yourself again, but this time you paid with your life," I pause. "I'm sorry. I'm sorry for hurting you, I'm sorry you felt like you had to put yourself in danger to protect me."

Tears well up in my eyes, then spill over like an endless river. I have experienced too much death in these past moons. I know my parents are dead. Nova is dead, and most of Ode's people are dead. To think that two power hungry Oderians could do this makes me upset. At least they won't do anything like this ever again.

"I should have trusted you. There were so many times when I didn't. I wouldn't be alive right now if it wasn't for you. I regret I didn't fix things between us sooner. I should have, but I was scared. I was scared of how I felt and of how you felt. I didn't want to ruin our friendship because of my stupid feelings. In the end, I realize not telling you was worse than telling you. I destroyed our friendship anyway. I should have been honest, after all, you were...most of the time. If I could go back and change things I would. I would make sure you were never captured and you never died. It really should have been me. This wasn't your fight. You were sucked into the mess. Plus, I became no better than a Constable. I killed the twins because they made me mad. They should have been brought to justice. You would have wanted that," I sigh.

I can hear the sound of the crowd outside. The roar of people weeping for their loved ones who sacrificed themselves so I could live deafens me. They gave their lives so I could become no better than the

Constables who hunted me down and tried to kill me.

I look back down at Nova, "I love you. That is one thing that will never change, no matter how much I try." I stand, turning to the open doors.

I glance at Nova one last time before I leave the temple. The doors close behind me, forever sealing him in with the stars. I stand at the top of the temple's steps, as I had stood on the steps of the Council dwellings after the war ended.

I make my way to the edge of the steps, the eyes of the people below trailed on me in silence. A silence I rather don't enjoy. Given the chance, I would have made a beeline to get out but these people needed to know who Nova really was.

"He saved us all," I say, my voice cutting through the air. "Without him, the rebels would never have made it through two attacks on the bases."

The people stare at me, some in tears, other gazing off into the distance sadly.

"However, I have many regrets. I quarreled with him too often, didn't listen when I should have and worst of all, I rejected him. I shunned him after I found out he had been a Constable," I continue. "I should have known though, he would be rash enough to do something like that. I hurt him. I hurt him by not accepting the fact he did it to keep me safe." Pausing, I let out a quiet sigh. "I have come to terms with his death by now, knowing even though it was the Council that sent him there, it was me who delivered the final blow. There were other ways to have handled it, but there was no time to waste. In the end, Ode was freed. He was not the only one we lost. I led your loved ones to their deaths knowing large numbers were going to die. There was no other way. I did what had to be done, and I accept the consequences of my actions. This world and your loved ones did not deserve that fate. For that, I am truly sorry."

I am afraid to look down at the people and see looks of horror at what I did. To me, it was almost as bad as what the Council did. So, I quit talking and walk down the stairs. Seginus joins me at the bottom. The silence of the crowd continues as I bring up the hood of my cloak, casting my face in shadow. I avoid their eyes as we walk until someone stops me, a hand on my shoulder.

"We do not blame you for the events that have occurred, consider yourself a hero," the man says, deep wrinkles are set in his face. He nods to me, a sympathetic smile settling itself on his lips.

I nod and mutter, "Thanks."

Glancing at Seginus beside me, he wraps his arm around me pulling me close as we set off again. Heading to the dwellings where the new members of the Council are about to be announced.

The new members will swear an oath to protect Ode and not let it fall into the destruction the previous Council did. They also added new positions, someone to represent each race that now lives on Ode, Oderians, humans, and even hybrids.

The downside to being the single hybrid to survive the war is that I'm the one person who can take that position as a leading member of the new Council.

Seginus and I stand near the front of the crowd, knowing when they call my name I must go up the steps to join the rest of the Council.

An Oderian reads off the list of new Council members before finally saying, "Our last member is the leader of the rebels, Commander Ara Rosette."

Seginus gives me a gentle nudge and a smile as I walk up the steps. Now everyone can move on.

Sometime later, after the new members had been released, I head home for the first time in many moons. I was afraid to come back so I stayed at the encampment the rebels made, but I now believe I am finally ready.

Chapter Thirty-eight

Ara

The streets of this area are deserted except for Seginus who sits alone waiting for me. I guess everyone left in fear of being captured and executed. I see no point in going into the house yet so I climb up to the roof and the night settles itself. Seginus silently climbs up and lies down next to me.

The stars above me gleam brighter tonight than I had seen them in a long time. Nova's last words echo in my mind, "So when you look up at the stars, from your roof, know the light shining down is my glow, keeping you warm. Keeping you safe."

I smile softly through the tears that forced their way out.

"Are you alright Ara?" Seginus asks quietly.

"I will be fine in time," I answer barely above a whisper. "I want to thank you Seginus."

"For what?" he turns toward me.

"Ever since Nova's kidnapping, followed by his death, you have helped me and been someone I can count on. I did love Nova, but it was never meant to be," I sigh.

He nods. "I was your second in command, nothing more. It was my duty."

"No Seginus, I am thanking you as a friend," I correct him.

He smiles at me. "No problem, Ara."

"I have one last request for you, Seginus, if that's alright?" I glance at him.

"Anything," he answers.

"I want you to stay with me like Nova did. You are the closest I have to a family, and right now I need someone," I request.

"I would gladly be your family if you will be mine?" he sighs.

"I will." I turn back to him. "Did you lose anyone during the war?" I ask, trying to learn a little more about him.

"I lost my little sister. My parents died a few moons before everything started. My sister, though, she was murdered by a Constable. That's why I joined the rebels, to do something she would have been proud of me for," he stares up at the stars as he speaks.

"How old was she?" I blurt out before I can stop myself.

"One hundred forty-four moons. She wasn't very old at all," he presses his lips together, "Did you have any siblings?"

I shake my head. "Only my parents and Nova. Of course, now they are all with the stars and all I have is you."

"People like us, we need to stick together don't we?" My heart flutters as his hand slides into my own.

There is no chance I can be with Nova now, but maybe I can move on and have a better life since I am no longer in constant fear of being killed.

"Yes, we do," I reply and nervously set my head on his chest, staring at the stars. "Nothing feels the same without Nova."

He runs a hand through my hair and says, "Nothing ever will."

I smile at him then look back up at the bright stars above us.

"I wish there was a way I could bring you back, Nova. At least a way to save you," I say out loud to myself and Seginus.

I jolt upright and Seginus jumps to his feet when we suddenly hear someone say, "What if there is?"

About the Author

A.M. Harris is a young author from Tulsa, Oklahoma. She has had a passion for writing since the first grade. This book actually started as a project for her seventh-grade reading class and she continued writing it on into high school. Not only does she love to write but she also enjoys music and plays flute in her high school marching band. She is a dedicated student and works hard to achieve her goals.

Made in the USA
Middletown, DE
08 March 2019